Paying For It

A Guide By Sex Workers For Their Clients

---

edited by Greta Christina

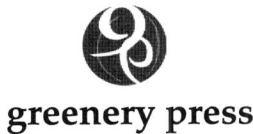

greenery press

Entire contents @2004 Greta Christina. Individual pieces copyright of the authors. All pieces original to this book, except for:

"Convoluted, Not Complicated," by Vic St. Blaise a.k.a. Lex Kyler, reprinted from his website, www.lexkyler.com.

"Samuel," by Annie Sprinkle, reprinted from Post-Porn Modernist, Torch Books, 1991; Cleis Press, 1998.

"The Session: From Phone Call to Graceful Exit," by Mistress Simone Worthington, reprinted from her website, www.chicagomistress.com.

"A Live One," by Greta Christina, reprinted from Penthouse Magazine, February 1997.

All rights reserved. Except for brief passages quoted in newspaper, magazine, radio, television or Internet reviews, no part of this book may be reproduced in any form or by any means, electronic or mechanical, including photocopying or recording or by information storage or retrieval system, without permission in writing from the Publisher.

Cover design by Johnny Ink, www.johnnyink.com.

Published in the United States by Greenery Press, 3403 Piedmont Ave #301, Oakland, CA 94611, www.greenerypress.com.

ISBN 1-890159-59-X.

Contents

Acknowledgments

First, last, and many times in between: Ingrid. A lot of people submitted very good work to this book, and I was genuinely sorry that there wasn't the space or budget to include all of it. So I want to thank, not just the contributors whose work ended up here, but everyone who took the time to submit their writing.

My friends and many members of my family listened to me patiently and gave me some very good advice while I babbled about this book incessantly for well over a year. I am very grateful to them for this. Ingrid in particular had to deal with anxiety attacks, mood swings, and a huge amount of what must have been very dull shop talk. I am more grateful to her than I can say. And special thanks go to Nicola for all the tech help. The manuscript would have been a mess without her.

Susie Bright has been a source of encouragement, inspiration, and excellent advice throughout my writing career, and as an editor has given me not only a ridiculously useful role model, but many of my most important breaks (including that all-important first one). She rocks.

I want to thank Last Gasp and all the Gaspers, for helping keep food in my belly and anarchy in my brain. On the subject of keeping food in the belly, I want to give special thanks to my father-in-law Russ. The "genius grant" meant a tremendous amount – the money was helpful, of course, but the vote of confidence was invaluable. And on this topic, I must thank Ingrid, once again and many times over.

Many of the contributors to this book are listed on the Eros.com Website, which is how I found them. Without it, this might well have been a very short book. Thanks.

Special thanks, of course, to Greenery Press, for giving an up-and-coming kid a chance. Extra special thanks to Patrick for the excellent advice on putting together the book proposal.

And last, first, and many times in between: Ingrid.

Dedication

For Ingrid.

Introduction

Why I Created This Book
– And Why You
Want to Read It

---

by Greta Christina

Some years back, a friend asked me for advice on visiting a peep show. He knew I had worked as a peep show dancer, and since he'd never been to one before, he didn't really know how to act. "Is it okay to smile?" he asked me. "Can I talk to the dancers? Should I compliment them? Or should I just watch and not do anything?"

It almost broke my heart. I thought about all those men who came into the Lusty Lady when I was working there, the ones who didn't smile or say hello or anything, the ones who just stood there and stared at my tits like zombies. All the time I'd worked there, and all the years afterwards, I'd always assumed that those guys were just jerks. And I'm sure some of them were just jerks. But when I was talking with my friend, I suddenly realized that a lot of those guys, maybe even most of them, were simply awkward or nervous or at a loss. I started wondering how many of them had wanted to say hello, or smile at me, or wave or wink or tell me I was sexy – and hadn't, simply because they didn't know whether it would be okay. It

---

occurred to me for the first time that some of those men had just stood there in the booth staring blankly, not because they were jerks, but because they didn't know what else to do.

And that's when I first thought of this book.

This book is somewhere between a consumer guide and an etiquette manual for sex work customers. It's meant to give customers a road map of sorts, to make them feel more comfortable when they walk into the peep show or the massage parlor or the dungeon, whether they've been there a hundred times or are just going in for the first time. The book is written by sex workers and former sex workers, female, male, and trans, who talk about how they do and don't like to be treated by their customers. The writers are (or were) prostitutes, strippers, lap dancers, peep show dancers, phone sex workers, professional dominants, professional submissives, "talk to a live nude girl" workers, and interactive Internet sex workers. Just about every type of sex work that involves direct customer interaction is represented in this book.

Here, you'll find a lot of things that sex workers want to say to our customers but don't feel that we can. We talk about what customers do to make us like them, and what they do to piss us off. We talk about customers who have made us feel relaxed, safe, appreciated, touched, and entertained; and we talk about customers who have made us feel frustrated, dehumanized, irritated, insulted, and threatened. And we talk about how differently we treat the first bunch from the second. In this book, you'll read story after story of sex workers who have given customers they liked a little extra attention – and who have given customers they didn't like the short end of the stick.

I edited this book because I think there's a vast and yawning communication gap between sex workers and sex work customers. For starters, customers often assume that sex workers lie to them. They assume that sex workers tell customers what they think the customers want to hear; that comments like "You're my favorite" or "I really have fun doing it with you" are just part of the standard bullshit rap. And this assumption isn't always wrong. Like any other job where politeness is a job requirement and getting repeat business depends on making customers think you like them, deception can often be a big part of sex work. It isn't always, but it can be.

For their part, sex workers often assume that customers don't particularly care about them or their well-being. They often assume that most customers are out for as much as they can get for as little money as possible, and that if a customer expresses caring or affection, it's a sign that he's a dupe or a nutcase or both, a self-deceived fool with an overactive fantasy life. And this assumption isn't always wrong, either. Much like customers in any business, sex work customers can often be deeply self-deceived and/or monumental jerks. They aren't always, but they can be.

There's also a common assumption that the exchange of money is proof that sex workers don't care about their customers, and that in fact they hold their customers in contempt for being pathetic losers who have to pay for it. Now, if you think about it for a minute, this is an awfully peculiar assumption. After all, you pay your doctor, or your therapist, or other professionals who provide very personal and intimate services, and you don't assume that they don't care about you just because you're paying them. For that matter, you pay your car mechanic, and you don't assume that she holds you in contempt because you "have to pay for it." So I'd like to put that assumption to rest right now. Sure, there are some sex workers who are contemptuous of their customers, just like there are some car mechanics who think their customers are idiots. And anyone who's worked in a job that caters to the public knows the behind-the-scenes eye-rolling over customers who are stupid or obnoxious or insane. But there's nothing about sex work that inherently instills its practitioners with derision for the people who seek out their service. The legal and social stigma notwithstanding, there's no reason sex work can't be like any other service industry, with no more mistrust and contempt between customers and workers than there is in any service relationship. (Admittedly, that might not be saying much, but it'd be a start.)

But as things stand, there's this communication gap. There's mistrust, there's misinformation, there's hostility and deceit, there's a relationship that's assumed to be adversarial by both sides. Not all the time, but a lot of the time. And when you throw in the social stigma, the legal vagaries, and the fact that sexual pleasure is a far more emotionally loaded service than a rebuilt carburetor or a cafe latte, you get a relationship that's often a minefield of suspicion and disappointment. My hope for this book is that it will help close the communication gap. The original title was "How To Treat Sex Workers So They Actually Like You Instead of Just Pretending To," and that's a big part of what I'm hoping for. I'm hoping to give sex customers a bit of a road map, to warn them away from some of the nastier land mines and point out some bridges over the chasm. I'm hoping to give customers some specific, practical ideas about what they can do to improve their working relationships, to let them know exactly how their behavior affects whether or not their sex worker likes them.

So why should you care if a sex worker likes you? After all, isn't that what you pay them for – so you can have sex with them (or spank them, or be spanked by them, or talk dirty with them, or watch them dance naked and fuck themselves with dildos) and not have to worry about what they're getting out of it? I know that attitude is true for a lot of sex customers. And odd as this may sound, I actually have a fair amount of respect for it. In the same way that I pay my therapist, at least partly, so I can talk about myself for an hour without having to stop and say, "But enough about me – how are you doing?," I think many sex customers pay so they don't have to stop and ask, "Do you like this? Is this turning you on? Is there something else you'd rather be doing?" They pay so they can get the sexual pleasure they want – sometimes a very specific kind of pleasure – without worrying about whether the other person wants it, too. And I think that's okay. You don't ask your car mechanic if there's something she'd rather be doing than replacing your fan belt, and I think you can have a perfectly decent and honorable relationship with a sex worker without worrying about whether he really gets off from crawling down a carpeted hallway rolling an egg with his nose. You don't have to treat sex workers as if they were your lovers – it's okay to treat them as professionals who are providing you with a service in exchange for money.

But there's a big difference between worrying about whether your sex worker is getting off sexually, and caring about whether your general behavior is annoying or insulting them. To draw a parallel: There's nothing wrong with going to a cafe and asking the waitress for a half-decaf latte with lowfat milk, extra foam, a shot of Torani syrup, and a sprinkle of cinnamon, even if she isn't in the mood and would really rather just give you a plain black coffee. But there is something very wrong with barking your order at her, calling her an idiot when she asks you to repeat part of it, losing your temper because it's taking her longer than plain coffee would, and not leaving a tip. So when I talk about getting a sex worker to like you, I'm not talking about the extra foam and cinnamon stuff. I'm not talking about getting them to like you as a lover. I'm talking about getting them to like you as a human being.

So we're back to the question: Why should you care if a sex worker likes you? Well, I hope that you'd care for the same reason that you care about your waitress (or your plumber, or your barber, or your piano teacher): because they're human beings, and you care about treating human beings with dignity and respect.

But if you want a purely selfish reason for treating sex workers well, I've got a great one for you. Sex work is like any other service industry: if the people providing the service like you, you're a lot more likely to get much better service. If the waitress likes you, she'll probably refill your water glass more often; if you're friendly and understanding with the customer service rep, he'll be more likely to give you a refund on the pants you returned, even if you sent them back two days after the return deadline. And the same is true for sex workers. If they like you, they're far more likely to go the extra mile, to give you special treatment or a little more service, or just to put extra care into making sure you're enjoying yourself. Even if the particular sex act you're paying for isn't something they do on their off hours, they still might have a pretty good time doing it with you if they think you're decent and pleasant – and if they're having a good time, they're a lot more likely to give you a good time, too.

The opposite, of course, is also true. Again, sex work is just like any other service industry: if the folks providing the service think you're an asshole, the best you're going to get is the bare minimum they're required to give you, and the worst you're going to get is thrown out on your ass. The waitress you leered at drunkenly is going to get to every other table before she gets to yours; the customer service rep you screamed at and threatened is going to stick like glue to the company's return policy and cut you no slack whatsoever. And the same is true for sex work. If a sex worker doesn't like you, they're very likely to give you a perfunctory blowjob, a tepid spanking, an uninspired lapdance, a phone call that's a minute less than you paid for. Even if they're professionals with high standards who take pride in their work and would never intentionally shortchange a customer, sex workers are human, and they're not going to be as attentive or inspired if they can't wait to get rid of you. And if they really, *really* don't like you, they may refuse to do business with you altogether.

I guess I should spell out something that's probably pretty obvious by now, which is that I think sex work is a valid and legitimate industry. I think it's a valid service to provide, and I think it's a valid service to pay for. I don't really have space here to argue that point as thoroughly as I might like; and anyway, it just seems obvious to me, so ridiculously obvious that trying to explain it leaves me sputtering for words. (If you want to see some writing that argues this opinion in more detail, read the excellent and ground-breaking anthology *Sex Work: Writings by Women in the Sex Industry*.) What it comes down to for me is that I don't have any problems with any mutually agreed-upon sexual relationship between consenting adults, and sex work is nothing if not a mutually agreed-upon sexual relationship between consenting adults. I've never understood why trading orgasms for money is supposed to be morally inferior to trading orgasms for orgasms – or for affection, or reassurance, or security, or companionship, or any of the myriad other reasons that people seek sex.

Obviously I'm opposed to anyone being forced into sex work against their will; and even more obviously, I'm opposed to sex work involving children. But that's because I'm opposed to rape and slavery and child molestation, not because I'm opposed to sex work. In a similar vein, I think it sucks when people are compelled by financial hardship to do sex work when they hate it. But a lot of people hate their jobs. Secretaries, factory workers, bookkeepers, store clerks, software testers, tollbooth operators... millions of people from all walks of life do work they don't like so they can keep food on the table, and it doesn't make the industries they work in inherently evil. The problem is social inequality, or an insufficient degree of economic mobility, or something – not the existence of the sex industries. At any rate, I've never understood how keeping sex work stigmatized (and in many cases illegal) is supposed to make things better for people who are forced into it by violence or threats or the fear of starvation. If anything, the legal and social marginalization of sex work makes things worse for these folks: it makes it harder to get out of the business, more dangerous to seek help from the police if they're being abused or defrauded, more difficult to find other work after they've quit. If you want to improve conditions for those sex workers who are being unambiguously and appallingly exploited, I think improving the legal and social status of all sex workers is a pretty good place to start.

Anyway. Off that soapbox for a moment, and onto another one. The point I want to make is that, while many sexually progressive people agree that sex work is a valid service to provide, there's not nearly the same support for it being a valid service to purchase. Even among people who are vigorously pro-sex-work, there's often a subtle (and sometimes not-so-subtle) contempt for the customers. This doesn't make much sense to me. I can't think of any other industry in which numerous people respect and value the providers while trivializing and despising the customers. So I'd like to state for the record that I think purchasing sexual pleasure is just as valid as selling it. I don't think the desire to pay for sexual pleasure is a sign that you're insensitive, or pathetic, or desperate, or emotionally stunted, or any of that. And I don't think the act of paying for sexual pleasure changes you into a person who's any of that.

This may seem like a contradiction. After all, there are some harsh words for sex customers in this book, including a few in the pieces I wrote myself. But I never would have edited this book if I didn't have compassion for sex customers. Heck, the whole premise of the book is compassion for sex customers. Its goal is to make sex work more pleasant and satisfying for customers (as well as for workers), and it's based on the assumption that a fair number of sex customers genuinely want a good, friendly working relationship with their sex workers and just don't always know how to make that happen. As a matter of fact, I've been a sex customer myself; not often, but I have put my quarters into the booth at the local peep show when I was hungry for the sight of a naked woman. And I don't think it turned me into a dehumanizing goon. Sex workers do have a number of valid gripes about some of our customers, and you'll read many of those gripes in these pages. But you'll also read about the good customers, the ones who brightened our days or enriched our lives, the ones we made a real connection with despite the minefield of stigmatization and mistrust.

Before I go any further, I'd like to strongly encourage you to read the whole book, and not just skip to the section that interests you. Even if you're strictly a phone sex customer and don't care about strip clubs, or you only visit pro dominants and would never pay for a blowjob, I still encourage you to read the whole thing. A lot of the advice that these writers give applies to lots of kinds of sex work, not just their particular field. The strippers have advice that's good for phone sex customers; the pro doms have advice that'll help customers of prostitutes; and so on. And don't be limited by gender or sexual preference, either. If you're a straight guy, you'll still want to read the pieces by the gay male workers, and vice versa. Some of the advice here is gender-specific, but most of it is good advice for everybody, and you should be able to screen out the stuff that doesn't apply to you.

Also, while this isn't really a safety book, I'd like to say a few words about safety anyway. When it comes to the kinds of sex work that involve direct physical interaction (i.e., prostitution and professional domination and submission), there are some health and safety risks, just as there are with any sexual interaction. I certainly don't buy the image of sex workers as careless, self-destructive disease vectors; sex workers may actually be more attentive to sexual safety and health than your average sexually active adult, since they're generally having a lot more sex. But as a customer, you still have to take responsibility for your own safety and well-being in an encounter with a sex professional, just as you do with an amateur. If you're going to have sex with a prostitute and they want to use a condom, use it and don't argue. If they don't insist on using a condom, use one anyway. If you're working with a professional submissive, learn how to do SM safely, so you can protect your sub from harm; if you're working with a professional dominant, learn how to do SM safely, so you can protect yourself from harm. There's a resource guide in the back of this book, listing books, organizations, and other resources relating to sex in general and sex work in particular, and it includes several resources that can give you info about sexual safety. (Of course, watching strippers and having phone or Internet sex are excellent forms of safe sex.)

And of course, here's the legal disclaimer. While many forms of sex work discussed in this book are legal in much of the U.S., some of them are not, and sex work laws vary from state to state and even from city to city. The editor, publisher, and contributors of this book are not advocating that anyone engage in any form of illegal activity, blah blah blah. We're just saying that *if* you choose, on your own initiative, to engage in activity that may or may not be illegal in your area, then we have some advice on how to do so in a way that will make the experience more enjoyable for everyone. We do strongly advise you to be aware of the laws in your area; the laws governing sex work are notorious for being vague, changeable, and unevenly enforced, and activities that are theoretically legal (such as stripping or professional domination/submission) may be interpreted as illegal by the local authorities if they're in a bad mood or it's an election year. So watch your back.

There's one last thing I'd like you to think about before I close this introduction. Many sex workers are writers or future writers, and many of us wind up writing about our experiences in the business. So the next time you're with a sex worker, keep this fact in mind. And think to yourself: If this person winds up writing about this encounter, what would I want them to say? Who do I want to be: the obnoxious jerk who did something so ridiculously awful the writer still remembers it years later, or the fun, thoughtful, imaginative sweetheart who totally made the writer's day? Who knows – this might be your legacy, the one thing that future generations will remember about you long after you're gone. Choose it wisely. And enjoy the book!

General Principles

What We All Agree On –
And What We Don't

---

by Greta Christina

So here's the thing. There are 32 pieces in this book, by 26 different writers. That's an entertainingly large heap of variety. There's writing here about lots of different kinds of sex work, more kinds than you might have even known existed, and the writers themselves are a pretty diverse bunch.

But there are some basic principles we all agree on. From the strippers to the dominatrices, from the four-figure courtesans to the forty-dollar-a-blowjob street workers, there are some experiences we all share, some guidelines that we all agree will help you have a better time with us. And that's what this book is all about, after all: helping you have a better time. So before you dive into the sea of impassioned opinion and detailed advice, I thought you might find it helpful to have an overview of the things we all agree on.

THINGS THAT ARE GOOD TO DO

Be upfront about what you want. Your sex worker wants you to be a satisfied customer – if for no other reason, they'd like you to come back. They want to give you the kind of sex play you want, and if what you want is something they won't do, they want to know beforehand, so they can send you on your way with no hard feelings (and maybe even send you to someone who's more compatible). It's very frustrating for us when a customer doesn't ask for what he wants and then sulks when he doesn't get it. (Phone sex workers are particularly eloquent on this subject.) So don't be shy, and don't worry about being selfish. If you clearly spell out what you're looking for, you're actually doing your sex worker a favor.

Now, you do have to be a bit careful here. While it's important to ask for what you want, it's also important not to be demanding. There's a big difference between making requests and giving orders. And you have to be extra-careful when you're dealing with escorts or other folks whose work is of questionable legality. To put it bluntly: You can call a professional dominant and say you'd like to be spanked with a spatula, and you can call a stripper agency and say you'd like someone in a cop uniform to take it off for your party. But if you call an escort and say that you'd like to lick their asshole and then get a blowjob, you're going to get hung up on faster than the speed of light. You can be more direct with escorts once you've seen them a few times, but if you're a first-time customer, you have to be more cagey and let them lead the way. So perhaps a more useful piece of advice would be: Ask for what you want up front, without being demanding, as clearly as you can without breaking the law.

Remember that sex workers are professionals. No matter how much your sex worker likes you, getting you off is still a job for them. For you, the encounter is a sexy treat or a bit of special companionship you indulge yourself with – but for them, it's their rent and groceries. They may like their job – many sex workers do – but it's still a job. Please remember this. I don't just mean that you should be extra-generous (although that certainly wouldn't hurt). I mean that you should accept the fact that money is part of the encounter, and you shouldn't be surprised or hurt when your sex worker wants to get paid. Don't expect dancers to spend time with you if you're not tipping; don't expect prostitutes or pro doms to give you freebies or discounts; don't expect phone sex workers to give you a few more minutes than you paid for. If you're a regular, they might offer you these or other goodies on their own initiative. But asking for it insults their professionalism, and it makes them feel like you don't think they're worth what they charge. You wouldn't ask your doctor or plumber to give you a free ride just this once, so don't ask it of your hooker or your stripper. And if you have an appointment, keep it, or call to say that you can't. Don't just flake and not show up.

Respect your worker's limits. There's this weird myth floating around that being a sex worker means never getting to say no. It's one of the more common images of sex workers – the picture of the helpless, desperate, endlessly compliant victim who has to do whatever you tell them because you're giving them money. It's like some twisted blend of a tragic figure and a hot slave-toy fantasy. And it's a load of horse potatoes. The reality is that most sex workers can and do turn down customers. They'll say no if they don't trust you, if they get a bad vibe off of you, and sometimes if they just don't like you. And they can and do turn down specific acts. A lot of sex workers have specialties, and all sex workers have things that are off-limits. So respect this. If there's something you want that they've said no to, accept it – either do something different with that person, or find another sex worker who's into your thing.

Bathe. I can't stress this enough. Every single sex worker that I've talked with, whether they've written for this book or not, has mentioned this. (Okay, obviously not the phone sex workers, but you get my point.) It's pretty basic, really: you're going to be in close physical contact with your sex worker, and you don't want to gross them out. Most sex workers don't give a damn about your weight, age, race, physical shape, physical ability, etc. – but they do care if you smell bad. If you want them to enjoy their time with you and give you their full attention, then you probably don't want them putting all their effort into not holding their nose. So take a shower before you see them. Don't try to mask it with heavy cologne, either; that's unpleasant in itself, and anyway it doesn't work.

Become a regular. This is one of the best, most positive things you can do to get a sex worker to like you and improve your time with them. Once you're a regular, your sex worker will trust you more; they'll know that you play by the rules (assuming that you do), they'll be more comfortable with you, and they won't be constantly on their guard. Plus they'll have a better idea of what you do and don't like, and they won't have to play Twenty Questions to get you where you want to go. So unless variety is the spice of your sex life and it's absolutely no good if it's not a different person every time, find someone you like and stick with them – if not all the time, then a lot of it.

THINGS NOT TO DO

Don't try to bargain your worker down from his/her stated price. Sex workers don't just find this annoying – they find it personally insulting. You may not mean it that way – you may just think you're practicing good, hard-headed business sense. But when you try to bargain, what a sex worker hears is, "You're not worth what you think you're worth." It sets up a combative relationship right from the start, and even if they let you get away with it, they're going to be resentful. And frankly, if you have a "Getting as much as I can for as little money as possible" attitude, you shouldn't be surprised if your sex worker takes a parallel attitude, and gives you as little as they can for as much money as they can take you for. If someone gives you a price that's outside your range, don't try to dicker them down. Just say "No thank you" and move on. (Please read Jorge Balça's "Sales, Bargaining and Discounts" on Page 22 for a more complete discussion of this principle.)

Don't push for stuff that your worker isn't willing to do. Magdalene Meretrix says it best: in her article on Page 17, she says, "When you visit sex workers, don't try to push them into being a different kind of sex worker than the one they chose to be." In other words, don't pressure a stripper to have sex with

you for money, and don't try to get a non-kinky escort to dominate you. You'll just piss them off. And even if you do manage
to convince them to go along (which isn't likely), you won't
have as good a time as you would with someone who actually
prefers to play your way. Figure out what you want from a sex
worker, and then find a sex worker who'll do that. You'll have
a better time with them.

Don't be drunk or stoned. Yes, you can have a drink at
the strip bar. But don't have six drinks. Heavy booze and drugs
doesn't make you charming – it just makes you think you're
charming. And it impairs your judgment. If you're hammered
or high, you're more likely to do things you'll regret later –
whether that's grabbing the stripper's crotch, saying "Yes, Mistress" to a harder flogging than you can take, or just blowing
more cash than you can really afford. Stay relatively sober.
You'll have more fun, and you'll remember it better.

Don't fall in love, or think you're falling in love. Before
I started work on this book, I had no idea this was so common. I'd actually had it happen to me – this one guy at the
peep show told me he loved me after watching me dance naked for thirty seconds – but I figured it was a fluke. Apparently
it's not a fluke. It happens to a lot of sex workers – women,
men, and trans, in every field of the sex industry. And it creeps
all of us out. People who fall in love with their sex workers
can act really inappropriately: they can get possessive, demanding of our time, jealous of our lovers and our other customers.
And even if you don't do any of that, the love thing still makes
us wiggy. You're taking what to us is a professional relationship and making it personal, and that can throw us for a serious
loop, not to mention crossing a boundary that's important to
us. So if you start falling for your sex worker, do yourself and
them a favor, and chill out.

THINGS I CAN'T HELP YOU WITH

After all that lovely clear advice, here's a note that may
drive you batty. Some of the advice in this book contradicts

other advice in the book. Not all sex workers like to be treated exactly the same way, what with them being individual human beings and all. So what do you do when one pro dom says, "Don't start playing the submissive role when we're just scheduling on the phone," and another says, "Give me a top's respect from the first moment you call"? How do you figure out what this particular person wants?

Well, it isn't much different from everyday life. (1) You can try educated guesswork, figuring out from facial expression, body language, and tone of voice how they feel. A tricky business, since many sex workers are very good actors and may be hard to read (not so different from people in your everyday life), but it's worth a try. (2) You can ask them. You may not get a straight answer – they may give you the answer they think you want to hear rather than the actual truth (again, not so different from the folks in your daily life) – but it's still worth a try. If you really want an honest answer, say so explicitly. "Is it okay if I ask about your personal life?" is a very different question from "Is it okay if I ask about your personal life? I'd really like to know; I know some people in your business don't like it, and I don't want to do it if it bugs you." (Once again, not so different from everyday conversation.)

But ultimately, you're just going to have to live with the fact that there's no way in hell that you can, or even should, please everybody all the time. Which leaves you with (3): Don't stress about it too much. Even the most well-behaved person in the world isn't going to please everybody all the time. (Look at the letters Miss Manners gets from people she's pissed off.) Do your best to treat sex workers with respect according to the guidelines in this book and your own standards of good behavior, and don't worry about whether you've figured out exactly what they want from you. After all, you're there to have a good time. You're paying to have a good time. And mostly, what your sex worker wants is for you to have a good time. So relax, and have one.

A Dash of Common Sense, A Pinch of Empathy

by Magdalene Meretrix

A former colleague used to tell clients, "The quality of your session with me depends on two factors: my mood and your attitude." Those two aspects are intimately connected. If you bring a bad attitude to your visit with a sex worker – prostitute, stripper, phone sex worker, pro dominant, or any other type of sex worker you can think of – their mood is going to plummet. If their mood is low, a good attitude can often cheer them up. A happy sex worker gives you a better show, better sex, better whatever-it-is they're providing. Now really, isn't that what you went to see them for in the first place?

But having a good attitude involves more than just being a nice guy. There are unwritten rules and taboos in sex work just like anywhere else. My aim is to save you and your sexual service providers a lot of grief by writing out some of those unwritten rules and filling you in about those taboos. Much of it is just common sense – but some of it might surprise you.

Possibly the number one complaint my colleagues and I have is poor hygiene. I hear a lot of complaints about attitude problems, but the problem of clients who smell bad is almost legendary in its scope. And while I'm speaking of Scope™, even the best groomed client can sometimes use a little mouthwash. It should just be common sense, but I'll say it anyway: Take a shower, brush your teeth, use deodorant. And please, if your worker has a bed, don't put your shoes on it! Don't use their hairbrush, their comb, their toothbrush... yes, clients have done all these things, to my colleagues and to me.

There's something else about hygiene that might not be so obvious. Cologne. Yes, yours smells lovely. But don't put so much on! Sex workers, especially those of us who work in high-traffic places like strip bars or brothels, get overwhelmed by odors all night long. It's hard for me to say which I dislike more – someone who hasn't bathed and comes in smelling of sweat, or someone who's put on so much cologne that I can barely breathe in his presence.

But I hate to sound like I'm lecturing you. I want to stop for a moment to say that the majority of clients are wonderful gentlemen: clean, neat, agreeable, and just pleasant to be around. So please don't think that I automatically assume you're going to be an irritating jerk. I don't, and neither do most of my colleagues. While we're always on our guard for the worst, we tend to expect the best of clients, and we usually aren't disappointed. The very fact that you're reading this book suggests that you're one of the "good guys" (the assholes don't care what we want, so I'm guessing they won't bother to read this). And I don't want you to feel that your kindness and good attitude aren't appreciated. Let me tell you right now: they are! But maybe you'll run across one little thing in this essay that you do that you hadn't realized was a problem – and, because you care, you'll try to change it.

So while I could talk about some very obnoxious things (like blatant insults, physical violence, refusing to pay and so on), I think we'll both be better served if I spend more time on the subtle things, things that even a considerate client might not realize were a problem.

You already know, of course, to treat your worker like a real person. Be polite, say "please" and "thank you," treat him or her with respect. But there is something we don't want you to do with us, even though it'd be okay with other people. It might hurt to hear this, but please don't fall in love with us!

It's the great paradox. We want to do our job well, but if we do, we sometimes make you fall in love with us – and we don't want that. Or perhaps I should say we don't want the behavior that tends to go along with that love. If clients who love us are still respectful of our boundaries, it's flattering and sweet. But too often that's not the case. A client might start by saying "I love you," which is harmless enough. But declarations of love are often followed by unceasing phone calls, demands on our time (especially on our free time), and ill-founded assumptions that we feel the same way about them.

So if you find yourself feeling overwhelmed by the desire to spend every waking moment with your favorite sex worker, slow down! Think things through. Above all, don't allow yourself to become a nuisance. It'll drive your sex worker away from you. And down the road, you'll just feel sheepish about how you behaved while under the spell of their charms.

You might think it would be okay to give gifts so long as you don't say "I love you" out loud. This is a sticky issue. Most sex workers I've talked to (myself included) have mixed feelings about gifts. We feel flattered and special when we get roses or chocolates or plush animals. But at the same time, there's a little voice in our heads that's asking us, "How much did these gifts cost? What bills could I have paid if he'd just given me the money instead? Roses smell lovely, but they don't put groceries on the table, do they?" It's a traitorous little voice, and hard to ignore.

If you really want to give your sex worker a gift, consider something like a gift certificate for books, CDs, or lingerie, so they can select what they prefer. Even better, just give that money as a tip, and write a lovely (but not too intense!) letter or poem. No, it's not very romantic, but you should never forget that while we're running a romantic business, we're not dealing in the business of romance.

Having cruelly shattered the romance bubble, I'll try to make it up to you with some specific pieces of practical advice.

When you visit sex workers, don't try to push them into being a different kind of sex worker than the one they chose to be. Let strippers remain strippers and don't try to make them into escorts. Let escorts be escorts and don't try to push them into being professional dominants or submissives. Your worker has chosen their line of work for a variety of reasons. Respect that.

Do follow your worker's lead in things. Let them show you what choice of wording you should use. Let them show you the right time (if any) to get physical. The more you can allow them to be in control of your time together, the better your time will be.

You should always let your worker know in advance about any disabilities or unusual qualities you have. It's for your own good as well – if they know, they may be better able to meet your needs. For example: If you're going to be pulling your dick out, and you have any kind of deformity like chordee (very bent penis) or extreme hypospadias (malformation of the urethra), let your worker know ahead of time so it's not a shock. It's only fair, really. Yes, they might turn you down as a client, but wouldn't you rather have a worker who knew ahead of time and accepted you anyway than one who felt pressured into accepting you?

And try to avoid behaviors that might alarm them. Talk a little bit – a totally silent client is creepy. If a stripper or escort is visiting your place, try not to have them show up at an apartment with no furniture. That's creepy, too. Remember that they're looking out for danger, so try to avoid doing anything that makes you look dangerous. They'll be a lot more comfortable, and you'll get a better, more relaxed session. And it's best not to alarm your sex worker unless you want to learn first-hand about their security measures!

If you call a stripper or an escort agency and they send you someone you don't choose to spend your money on, be sure to give them gas money. It wasn't their fault that they didn't make your cut. And don't come into a sex work establishment with "the guys" if you know you're going to wind up sitting around in a group making insulting jokes about the workers and not spending any money. (Admit it – you know that's what generally happens when you all go out drinking in the strip bar together!)

Finally, be appropriate with sex talk. If you're with a pro dom, a phone sex worker, or anyone else whose line of work isn't against the law, or if you've gone to a Nevada brothel or some other place where paid sex is legal, co be explicit about what you want so you have a chance to get it. But if you're talking to the escort agency on the phone, don't be explicit at all! You will get hung up on for fear that you're a cop. It may seem confusing, trying to figure out when you can talk about it and when you can't. But when in doubt, revert to the earlier rule: follow the sex worker's lead.

I hope that all your encounters with the professionals who work hard to make you hard are smooth and satisfying, and that you leave all your service professionals thinking, "What a wonderful gentleman he was!" A measure of common sense combined with a modicum of putting yourself in someone else's shoes should be all it takes. Many happy returns to you!

Sales, Bargaining and Discounts

by Jorge Balça

Throughout my five years working in the sex industry, bargaining has always been an unpleasant constant. If the mercenary side of offering one's body and soul in a commercial transaction can be the least pleasant part of it, debating what one is worth in terms of figures is often insulting, tiresome and fruitless.

While the process of hiring professional companionship (apologies for the euphemism) follows the same basic principles of any other commercial transaction, one should bear in mind that the merchandise is by nature substantially different from any other. Trying to get the best price in any commercial transaction is in our capitalist nature, but a bit of thought can easily explain why so many sex workers of all sorts – escorts, dominants, submissives, dancers, and so on – grow cold and even unpleasant when a discount is asked for.

The problem is that bargaining can very easily be interpreted as an insult, even where none is intended. The object of the transaction is the sex worker him/herself: his/her body and personality. When a client tries to argue that the stated rate is too high, what's really being said is that the sex worker is not worth the amount stated. And although it may be okay to think that, what good will come of saying it? Sex workers are wary of clients indulging in lengthy discussions about fees. "If the client disrespects me in this matter," they think, "chances are that he/she will do the same in other aspects as well." Embarrassment and discomfort to both parties can easily be avoided if the bargaining process is skipped altogether.

Of course, there are situations in which the rate is simply too high for the client's pocket. But wouldn't it be more polite to simply state that the rate cannot be afforded, instead of implying that the rate is too high for what's being offered? This will allow the sex worker to be courteous when thanking the client for the interest shown, and leaves the option open for a future relationship. Furthermore, clients should bear in mind that hiring a sex worker, especially a more expensive one such as an escort or a professional dominant, is a lot closer to buying a luxury item than going to the local market. In fact, one should beware of anyone in the sex industry who seems unsure or too flexible regarding their rates. Uncertainty of rates probably means uncertainty of service quality.

Discounts or special rates may be considered by the sex worker after a rapport with the client is established. After a few meetings, or if the client becomes a regular, the sex worker may decide to offer a special rate, or a discount for a particular encounter. But as with any gift, expecting it or asking for it is rude and counterproductive.

Ultimately, sex work is all about making someone's fantasy come true. What is being offered are fantasies on tap. A clear arrangement of rates and an honest discussion about what is required will result in a more enjoyable experience for both parties, without the anti-climax of an awkward discussion about what the fair amount due is. The sooner the set-up is agreed on (preferably before meeting), the sooner the fantasy can start.

Advice for Anyone Who Sees A Sex Worker in Person, And In Particular For Dominatrices' Male Submissive Clients Who Want to Be Tied Face to Face (or More Accurately, Face to Chest) with Said Dominatrices' Paid Female Submissives, While Both Subs Are Beaten or Spanked or Whatever

by Koko

Bathe.

Prostitutes

Memo to My Clients: How to Keep Your Job

---

by Carol Queen

I worked as a call girl for about ten years (depending on how you do the math), and by the end of that time I had fired most of my long-term clients and only saw my favorites. Since most clients were not long-timers and I fired a fair number of guys, that only left a handful of men I'd been seeing for years and was willing to continue to see.

I got into the biz when I was over thirty and already knew my way around my own body. I was in an exciting and intense period of erotic exploration, and prostitution was certainly part of that (though by no means the most exciting part – I had a partner at home with whom I swung much harder from every possible chandelier). This is not to say that when a client came by I was just clocking in, or thinking about England, or waiting for the hottest part of the encounter – the slowly-revealed wallet. No, when I liked someone, I played for real, and many clients liked that about me. I was always a little bemused about the clients who didn't seem to notice. It made me wonder if anyone had ever pulled out the stops with them, paid sex or no.

I was not a typical prostitute – but there is no typical prostitute. It's very hard to generalize about street 'hos and

---

call girls, boy escorts and tranny hookers, bar and brothel workers, and all the other ways the oldest profession plays out in America and around the world. If you make assumptions and listen to stereotypes, you're going to get it wrong. So the fact that I was highly educated, enjoyed the work on most days, and felt it suited not only my bank account and schedule but also my personal philosophy, and the fact that my background held none of the abuse some researchers-with-an-attitude always seem to find (funny, they never survey me and my friends) – this is all relevant to my experience only, and you can't generalize it to all other sex workers. But the category of Sex Workers does include people like me, as well as people who are very different.

(Can you tell I have a degree in sociology?)

So as I was saying, as I began to wind down a decade-long sojourn in the Valley of the Blowjobs, I fired a number of my clients. I did it first because I had begun to get a little burned out. In the very beginning of my callgirlhood, I had done nothing more strenuous off the job than write and fuck my brains out off the clock. I had plenty of downtime between visits from clients, didn't usually have to rush, and lived a fairly mellow existence. By the time ten years had passed, I had a day job, deadlines every week, and a partner I was sharing space with – space we had to negotiate, since almost no client wants to pay for quality time with someone whose sweetie is popping in and out of the room. And on a monthly basis I rushed out of town for a speaking gig or workshop tour. Fitting clients into this schedule – especially those clients who didn't want to wait three weeks for me to have a couple of available hours – was stressful. On top of all this, I had come out in print as a prostitute, which meant that any new client might be from the police department – on duty, not off.

So I was stressed. I needed to simplify. And the first thing to go was my client (I'll call him John) who had gotten so attached to me that he'd begun to pry into my private life. He didn't begrudge the money he paid me every week, but he didn't seem to regard it as pay for play, either. An older guy, recently widowed, he'd come up in an era when men mostly had to shell out something to get next to a girl – and I think that in his mind, the two hundreds he included in the weekly Hallmark card were just a little gift that would help keep me in shoes. He took me to dinner every week after our session; he was clearly in it for the companionship, which was fine. He was pleasant to talk to, not a bore, and he let me choose the restaurants.

But talk turned to what I did when he wasn't around, and I (not having met a client like him before) saw no reason not to talk about my life. Big mistake! He got increasingly jealous of my full-time relationship, and urged me to drop my partner. As it dawned on him that I did this with all the guys, his sweet and devoted demeanor changed. He got chilly – and he wanted me to show him all kinds of new sex tricks. Ordinarily this would have been part of the fun, but this time we were doing it because he "wanted to get what he was paying for." I fired him.

Dear reader, do not make the mistake of thinking the sex worker is your girlfriend/boyfriend, or will shortly yield to your many charms. Do not pester her about what she does with the other 167 hours in her week. Do not forget that, even if the callboy is very sweet to you, it is in his economic best interest to keep you coming back for more. He's not your new lover. In short: Respect the boundary between yourselves that your respective roles as client and sex worker create. Within those boundaries, you can get hot, have fun, and even be affectionate.

Corollary: If your professional seems to be inviting him/herself into your life on a boundary-free basis, make sure you are that rare twosome – a customer/pro pair who can make the transition to "real" life. It's not unheard-of – but mostly, it's a bad idea. You may soon be in a position to sacrifice, not just the contents of your wallet, but your bank account and your heart as well.

Boundaries also include what kind of sex your professional will have with you. Never, ever buy into that awful phrase, "selling your body." We sex workers do not sell our bodies. We ask you to pay for our time. That time guarantees an opportunity to negotiate for the kind of sex you want. It doesn't guarantee *getting* the kind of sex you want. And it certainly doesn't guarantee that, at your whim, we'll dispense with condoms or other safety-related practices. Don't pester us about it, and don't whine about it. Don't you understand that if we leave the condom in the drawer for you, we might have left it in the drawer for the last guy, too? Two words, my friend: Pleasure Plus, the brand of condom favored by more men than any other. (Buy your own, they're expensive.)

I was always pleased to open my door to clients who knew what they wanted when they came to see me. The ability to be clear about their desires made us able to talk about those desires and decide how our session was going to go, with little trouble (usually). Then we could get right to it. Some guys, on the other hand, appeared to want something other than blowjobs and fucking – but what? Gentlemen (and those few intrepid ladies who call us as clients), we do not have time in an hour to try every damn thing in *The Joy of Sex*. If you don't give us at least a teeny hint, we will need many sessions of trial and error to figure out what your turn-on is. And believe me, most of us would like you to go away pleased. Our professional pride is bruised when you won't let us do our best. So communicate! Maybe you can't tell your wife or girlfriend what you want, but the cat doesn't have to get your tongue when you pay for it.

My clearest communicator, ironically, is one of the guys I fired – but I only fired him near the end of my time in the business. Reason: He was *so* clear about what he liked that we only ever did the exact same thing, every single session I ever had with him. I could set my watch to the point at which he'd flip me over for doggy style, and I could have won large sums of money placing bets on what he'd say right before he came. He was like a wind-up toy, bless his heart! But when I first met him, I was truly impressed by his devotion to his exact favorite scenario. He was completely clear about what he wanted.

So was my all-time favorite client – but the difference between the two men couldn't have been more vast. This guy (I'll also call him John) was obviously comfortable with his body and with sex. He represented the sex work client in it for the fun, relaxation, and pleasure. Maybe at home he was frustrated and locked out of his wife's affections, but I doubt it. I think he was just a friendly and pleasant guy who liked sex and liked variety. He was fun to fuck, didn't keep me guessing, and could chat about any topic. Social skills and a nice dick: he was just swell. I came to know his sexuality well enough to know what would get him off. But he did like variety, and over the ten-plus years I saw him, we moved gradually through different kinds of play. "I think maybe next time I'd like to get fucked with a strap-on," he'd say, giving me plenty of time to lay in a new set of toys.

I tended not to watch the clock too hard as a prostitute; I wasn't working in a brothel, after all, and if it took a client a little longer than an hour to come, I wasn't going to reach for his wallet in the middle to make sure he had enough for another hour. But with this John I was especially willing to take time, because it was fun and friendly and pleasant.

I recall another guy who was so uncomfortable that I was in an absolute rush to get him out of my apartment. Was he at war with self-hatred about his own sexual impulses? Was he giving himself shit because he "had to pay for it"? (And how many guys indulge in dark moods for having to pay for food at restaurants when they're hungry?) Or did he disrespect me for selling it? I don't know, but he and the few guys like him were among the worst experiences I had as a call girl. Guys, if you feel horny, what's wrong with a quick wank in the employee rest room? It's a challenge for any sex worker to give good service to a client who, for any reason, hates being served. And clients like this don't get their money's worth, because they can't enjoy what they get.

This goes for all the clients who think sex workers are somehow lesser beings because we do the jism-stained work of orgasm and release. Guys, you come to us for a reason – get comfortable with it! And respect us for what we do for you. Sure, you have a pure Madonna at home, the mother of your babies, your beloved angel. I'm sure she's a doll, fella, but if she won't blow you and you want to get blown, leave the bad attitude outside my door. Appreciate me for what I do, or you're wasting your damn money.

And if you get a deep-down feeling that your pro doesn't respect you, even though you're doing your respectful and pleasant best, consider finding another pro. Not everyone is cut out for this, you know. Without any disrespect to them – they have their reasons – plenty of sex workers are burned out and have bad attitudes. "Be nice to prostitutes," as Scarlot Harlot's bumper sticker says – but no one at the Better Business Bureau will fault you for looking for someone who is nice in return. After all, a large component of sex is skin-to-skin fellowship – not intimacy, necessarily, but plenty of clients see prostitutes to get their touch needs met, and those needs are better-met when the provider can make you feel comfortable and welcome.

My best client experiences didn't have to do with cock or wallet size. They involved a sense of comfort and fun. These elements of a client/pro exchange are probably absent for those clients – and prostitutes – who cannot respect themselves. So that may be the most important rule of all.

Oh, just one more thing. Wash your smelly balls before I bury my nose in them, dear, unless we negotiated that you could come to bed sweat-soaked and clammy. The sink is right over there.

Convoluted, Not Complicated

by Vic St. Blaise, a.k.a. Lex Kyler

I heard Margo St. James, the founder of COYOTE and the St. James Infirmary, say this about prostitution: "It's not complicated. It's convoluted, but not complicated." So it goes for proper etiquette in hiring sex workers. I hope to smooth out some of the bumpiness with my perspective and a few tips. With practice, you can enjoy the most from your encounter by using respect, clarity, preparation and balance as your tools.

The Golden Rule didn't earn its reputation by hiring an image consultant. It really works. If you can remember only one thing – to treat the worker as you'd like to be treated – you can't go wrong. Respect is essential – respect for boundaries, for privacy, for space for your hired help to work with. Respect is one thing sex workers don't get enough of, not even from other guys in the business, so when we encounter some, we really appreciate it.

Clarity is one of the advantages (along with convenience, attention, and expertise) that a pro sex worker leverages over amateurs. For the worker, it means knowing what you are willing to offer, stating your availability, and cutting out a lot of the games that typify the sexual hunt. For the client, clarity means knowing what you are looking for, and what is not acceptable. Keeping defined boundaries does not mean sucking all the spontaneous air out of your session; rather, it is a structure to build on.

Clarity is not to be confused with disclosure. Unfortunately our service is still criminalized, and anything we say or type can be used against us. How much we state about what we will do for X amount of dollars... that depends on our comfort level, or our naiveté. Still, before going ahead with setting up an appointment, you should be clear about your needs and believe that they will be attended to.

Preparation minimizes any glitches that might interrupt your pursuit of happiness. If you're ordering in, make sure that your home or hotel is in a pleasant condition, and that you have the necessary condoms, lube and whatever else you want to use during the session. If you're traveling, give yourself enough time to get there, find parking, and go to a cash machine.

Oh, and give yourself time to clean out. One of the most common complaints, and a guaranteed soft-on, is the customer who is not clean where he needs to be. It's doubly important because it's a matter not only of preparation, but of respect. Do you want to be remembered as the guy who left skid marks on the sheets? (And wasn't that a tactful, PG-rated way of saying "douche your fuck hole"? Try slipping that phrase past the AOL thought police.)

You already incorporate balance in your everyday decisions, and it serves you well. There's no need to abandon it in the frontier world of compensated sex. You may already know this too well, but anyone can declare himself an escort, just as anyone with enough cash can hire. Like so much of this business, the open road is a source of excitement, as well as risk. But balance will aid you in your risk assessments in choosing a companion, as well as dealing with him in the naked flesh. Your worker is doing a multi-balancing act as well, juggling reality with fantasy, intimacy and boundaries, and other things

I'm sworn not to reveal. Use balance as a lubricant to give you and your worker room to play, to add some of that exciting unknown to a session, and as a cushion for any expectations waiting to turn into resentments. With good manners and practice, you will learn how to stay clear of unpleasantness.

And another bit of business to get out of the way. (Did you think I meant cash? That's pretty straightforward, file that under clarity.) I mean opting out. As you'll see, it's easy at first and gets progressively trickier, but that doesn't mean you should do anything you don't want to do just because money is involved. Rejection isn't fun for anyone, we workers have feelings too, but at some point you may want to exercise your choice to say no. We'll get to that later.

Here is a list of specific tips, including which of your basic tools will help you:

Before you crack open a paper, run a search engine, call an agency, or drive to a stroll, decide what your needs are (clarity).

Think about what attributes you'd like in the guy you hire, but do leave some wiggle room, and don't get hung up on stats. Everyone expects us to play with the figures, so we oblige (clarity, balance).

Find out as much as you can about someone who interests you before you make contact. Read the whole ad, visit their website and read all of it, or ask the dispatcher questions (preparation).

Simply don't contact anyone you have no interest in hiring (respect, opt out card).

Never contact a professional in hopes of getting a freebie (respect). Only other workers are allowed to do that, and even then, it's done under the guise of finding work partners/trade.

If you're paging an escort, give him a chance to return your call before you get on the phone with your next choice. To a worker, a busy signal means a prankster or some guy shopping for the cheapest deal, and we don't like that (respect).

Avoid probing questions, and temper your language and requests. Explaining what you're looking for and asking if that's of interest is far better than "how much for a blow job?" If you're not satisfied that you two are on the same page, politely thank him and move on without comment (balance, respect, opt out card).

Respect a worker's privacy requests. This extends to not providing birth names, face pictures, x-pics, and home addresses (respect).

Never treat the person you're contacting as if he was running a yard sale. Or, more bluntly, no haggling – ever (respect, respect, respect).

If you find out something about the guy that's not acceptable and non-negotiable, and it's something that can't be changed (such as height to weight ratio, penis size, hirsuteness, age, etc.), politely thank him and move on without comment (respect, opt out card).

Each worker takes his own approach to the business. Some are willing to negotiate activities, length of session, even fees. But proceed with caution, and make sure there's agreement before you proceed (clarity, balance).

Don't try to blind us with wildly unrealistic scenarios and vast sums of money – we don't believe you. A four-hour session? Make an appointment and a cash deposit. Want to fly someone out for a weekend? Send a cash deposit so the worker can make his own arrangements. Or better yet, fly yourself to his home turf and take a one-hour test drive to see if you're compatible (balance, respect, common sense).

Turn off your television before dealing with an escort (respect).

Stick to your appointment, treat it like a contract. If your Man A calls back after you've already made arrangements with Man B, thank A and tell him you'll try him again in the future (respect, karma).

Shower, shave, and douche to avoid smells, stubble and skidmarks (preparation, respect).

Avoid cologne. It drives some of us crazy, and not in a good way (preparation, respect).

Nothing is more universally flattering to a man's feet than white gym socks (preparation).

If you're going out, arrive at the destination on time: not early, since we're still sexing up our apartment, and not late (preparation, respect).

If you're entertaining, votive candles beat all other forms of lighting, especially in hotels (preparation).

Have a good story ready and an envelope with a kill fee in case you meet him and your gut tells you this was a mistake (preparation, respect, opt out card).

If the guy who shows up at your door really does not match his description or photo, you might consider telling him so and not giving him a kill fee. Sure, and he might be the kind of person that could give kill fee a new meaning. I once heard that customers don't pay us to come, they pay us to leave. Apply it here (balance, preparation, peace of mind).

Money first or after? There is debate about what is proper. If it's after midnight and you've indulged in some party favors, definitely money first. Before midnight and you're somewhat sober, an open envelope stuffed with bills someplace where it will be noticed will suffice (preparation).

If you think your needs are specialized enough to warrant an explanation, feel free to review what you'd like before you start your session (clarity).

Use positive reinforcement along the lines of "Oh, that feels great" and "God that's good" and compliments like "You look even better in person" and "Go slow, that's a lot bigger than I'm used to" to heat up your session. We're looking for cues rather than instructions, and will adjust to your feedback (how to win friends and influence people).

Exercise caution should you decide to give out directions during sex. These can easily be interpreted as orders and judgments — sure soft-on producers. If there's something specific you want, word it as a suggestion or request (balance).

If you're at a hotel, answer in your bathrobe or naked (clarity, it puts us at ease that you're not the law).

Start undressing right away (clarity, puts us at ease that you find us hot).

Don't pressure your model to orgasm. Our job is to do our best to help you have yours, and pressure has an unfunny way of producing soft-ons because it distracts us from our job. If a cum shot was previously agreed upon before, still, let it happen on its own. You can lead a horse-hung rock, but you can't squeeze semen out of it (respect, balance, mangled proverbs).

Calling out your hired man's name during orgasm is always correct, but keep the volume appropriate, especially if you're at his place (flattery, balance).

Spend some time recuperating, but let your man know you don't want to be selfish and keep him from all the other men who want to see him. Sometimes we don't mind staying longer than planned, but sometimes we do have other things to attend to (like laundry).

If at the end of the session you really want to see this guy again, give him a tip – and remember how much, as he'll expect the same amount next time (respect, preparation).

If you want him hot and ready each time you see him, keep upping the tip. It stimulates us to do more to stimulate you (formerly well-kept secret).

If you're visiting his "office," leave pleasantly and quietly. Also, should a friend or neighbor pass by and call him by his real name, let it slip in one ear and out the other unnoticed (respect).

That's plenty to take in, and I'll let that innuendo slide in and out on its own power without any assistance from me. Good luck in your adventure. I wish you all the best.

On the Street

by Joy James, interviewing Stephanie

My girlfriend's name is Stephanie. But that's not her real name. It's her street name. Even though I consider her a girlfriend, she's never told me her real name, and I've never asked. That's the way it is on the street.

I've worked the street a few times. Just to see what it was like, I told myself, but it can become addictive. For Stephanie, it's now a way of life. It's her job, the way she supports herself and her two-year-old baby boy, Jason. When she's on the street, Jason stays with her mother, who's not sure exactly what Stephanie does for a living. However, Stephanie suspects her mother suspects. That much Stephanie has told me.

We really don't say much that's meaningful, but we do talk a lot while standing on the corner waiting for tricks. Really, she was the only girl who befriended me when I first tried out the scene. She was standing alone, unlike the other girls, who tend to group in clusters.

You get more action alone, she said. Men are sometimes intimidated by groups. But it's a trade-off. Alone there's more risk, while there's a certain safety in numbers. If a girl doesn't come back from a ride with a trick, the other girls in the group can report it – if not to the police, at least to their pimp.

Not all the girls have pimps. Stephanie doesn't. But there's constant pressure to get one. Just the few times I've worked the streets, men would approach me. Not in slow-moving cars, like the tricks, but always on foot. "Hey, gorgeous, haven't seen you around. What you up to?" That's something they'd typically say, while looking you up and down, then fixing you in the eyes with an unblinking stare.

They weren't necessarily menacing, but they were plenty persistent – checking me out, sometimes using a cell phone to tell someone on the other end what I looked like, then letting me know that some lucrative business could be mine. Throughout the night they would return, talking to me some more. After a while, Stephanie told me, most girls just get worn down and decide a pimp is better than the continuous hassle.

There's also hassle from the cops, of course. It comes in two forms. The first is serious, when they're intent on making arrests. They play undercover with unmarked cars and all that jazz, just like on TV. A girl has to be careful. So don't take offense if the street worker you're trying to pick up seems to be playing a game of Twenty Questions. She's trying to just make sure you're not really a cop.

The other type of police harassment is mostly for show. If there's too much action on a particular block, they'll try to clear it out. With the police cruiser's light flashing, they'll scare everybody off, particularly the guys cruising the neighborhood looking for action. They'll suddenly speed home to be with the wife. But savvy guys get a feeling it's all for show, and simply drive a few blocks away until things calm down. Then it's back to business, and life goes on. Sometimes the police will play their little game again, a couple of hours later, to show complaining residents and businesses that "something is being done" about this so-called blight on the neighborhood. At least, that's the way it is in D.C., with whose streets I'm familiar. Sometimes when the citizen complaints get too bad, the police really crack down, and the street workers in that particular area are effectively put out of work. The only option is to move to another area. So if you can't find us at our usual hangouts, just ask around. We've probably just set up shop a few blocks away.

Another thing that often tends to freak out customers is the presence of social-worker do-gooder types. Don't worry about them. They're not moralists and won't take down your license plate number or anything. They're just handing out free condoms and business cards – the latter should any of us street workers wish counseling. Street work can be hard, and it takes its toll. It's helpful if customers realize this and treat us accordingly.

In other words, please don't make it any harder. We're here to serve, and as in any service industry, the job satisfaction depends on the customers. Some can be jerks. But it's not in your self-interest to be a jerk, since workers have good memories and word travels fast on the street.

I'll never forget one guy, for example. He slowly drove his car around the block a few times, then parked it on the corner with the engine running. Stephanie warned me that he was trouble, but I was the new girl on the block and didn't listen. So I sauntered over to his car and stuck my head in the open passenger-side window. No sooner did I notice that his cock was already whipped out and he was jerking off, then he let fly a huge wad across the seat, almost hitting me in the face. That's apparently how he got his jollies. And I got nothing.

So the first – really only – rule of etiquette is simple: If I make you get off, I should get paid. Otherwise, you're stealing.

You can try to negotiate the price. That's the American way. Haggling is what the free market is all about. It all comes down to supply and demand. If it's a cold winter's night and my legs are shaking in their thigh-high leather boots and micro-mini, and there are too many girls on the street and not enough tricks, I might let you bargain me down.

But don't get mad if some girls won't wrangle. Stephanie, for instance, never deviates from her flat rate of $40 for a blowjob. It's a matter of principle to her. That's the bottom line value for her service from which she'll never waver. If you don't like the price, there's no hard feelings. Just drive on and try another girl. There's no need for insults or threats.

Just keep things businesslike. That's the most important thing to remember. The street worker you contract with is your business partner. That's the best way to look at it. If you think you're slumming and treat her like a low-life, than all you're really doing is making a statement, not very pretty, about yourself. And the girls on the street will respond in kind.

Try to act like a gentleman (even if you're not), and treat her like a lady. Sure, you can talk dirty and call us sluts if that turns you on. That doesn't mean you can't be polite. And who knows? – we might just thank you with some special added value, free of charge. Call it a reverse tip.

Case in point: For one regular, Stephanie no longer insists on a rubber, and then at the end, simply because he loves it so, she swallows. "A scholar and a gentleman," that's what Stephanie calls him, the exact opposite of a jerk or a bastard. He can't get enough and keeps coming back, at least once a week, for more. He's an educated professional: you can tell by the way he talks and dresses, plus the car he drives. But most importantly, he treats her like a true lady, and not just a lady of the night. So she knows (or believes, anyway) that he's not only a gentleman but clean and disease-free as well. Street workers have a sixth sense about these things. (For true insight into human nature – and the old adage that "it takes all kinds" – just work the streets for a few nights!)

Although working the street does have a bad reputation, the reality is that all the girls are just trying to make a living. Sure, some might have drug problems or come from unhappy homes or whatever, but that doesn't alter the fact that they are providing a service you value enough to part with your own hard-earned money for. So don't be a jerk about it. If you treat us as you would any other business partner – with at least some degree of politeness and respect – the transaction should lead to the happiest of outcomes.

In point of fact, few street workers view themselves as being on the bottom rung of the sex industry's hierarchical ladder (the all-too-common assumption). Rather, it's a highly personal choice, often based on predilection, convenience, and simple economics. A good night can be very lucrative, frequently better than escorting. And you can hit the streets when you feel like it, not at the whim of a phone call from your escort agency. Invariably the agency's call comes when you're in the middle of something else, and the farthest thing from your mind is sex. But when you get all dressed up to hit the streets, in the most provocative clothes you wouldn't dare wear anywhere else, the only thing on your mind is sex.

Yes, I'm in the mood. Don't ruin it by being a jerk!

Tips for Tricks

by Mattilda, a.k.a. Matt Bernstein Sycamore

F irst of all, remember: Just because you're paying
  doesn't mean that you can do whatever you want. As with
any sexual encounter, sex with a whore involves consent. This
means that no, you can't just slip it in without asking, or say
Oops when you "accidentally" slide your dick into my asshole.

Don't ask what I do "for a living." I'm a whore – remember?

Don't ask if I'm HIV-negative and STD-free. If you're
interested in staying safe, then make sure you take the necessary precautions. I always do. Similarly, don't ask me if
I'm "clean" – HIV-positive people are not dirty, and clean
people get STDs all the time. If you want information about
HIV and STDs, I'd be glad to counsel you as to the risk
factors involved with various behaviors. In my experience,
tricks who ask me if I'm negative are usually the ones who
want to fuck me without a condom. Years ago, I was getting a routine STD screening and tested positive for rectal
gonorrhea even though I had never – to my knowledge –
been fucked without a condom. I realized that this one trick
had slipped off the condom without asking. Since then, I
generally don't trust tricks to fuck me. If you want to have
a fun time, start by respecting me.

Get over your realness fetish. Sex work is all about illusion. I'm perfectly willing to satisfy whatever fantasy you have in mind, but I really wish you wouldn't ask me if I am "really" clean-cut, straight, bisexual, in college, "just doing this for fun," or any other simplistic scenario. If you want me to be any of these things, just ask me to indulge your fantasy. If you want me to be butch, you don't have to ask me if I'm "really" masculine. Hookers are masters of illusion.

Always wash before you're meeting a hooker. Brush your teeth and use mouthwash. I've met way too many tricks with hygiene problems – and no amount of cologne can disguise this. In fact, the only thing worse than an unwashed trick is a trick who smells of way too much cologne. There is no need to perfume your pubes – I'd rather my face smell like dick then Tommy, anyway. Soap will work just fine.

Don't ask me to bareback, fuck "raw," or go "all the way." Don't tell me this is "natural" or that you just want to be close to me. If you want to be close to me, give me a big tip.

Always tip. It's amazing what a couple of extra twenties can do. Don't ask for change – that's obnoxious.

Don't ask how many times today I've seen clients, how many clients I see in a week, how long I've been a whore, how I got started, or any other questions that are guaranteed to be answered with lies.

If you need to change your plans at the last minute, make sure to take both of our needs into account. Remember, I'm not turning tricks just to pass the time – this is the way I make my living. Always call if you're not going to show up. I can't tell you how many tricks just assume that it's okay to flake. And if you do have to cancel, be sure to make up for it with an extra tip at the next session.

Don't ask what I do when someone completely hideous comes to the door. We both know that person could very well be you.

Figure out what you want before I arrive. This is the best way for us to have fun, and for you to be satisfied. I do have a great intuition, but I am not clairvoyant. Don't tell me to do whatever I want – I want to get paid and leave.

If you want me to be your therapist, just ask. I'd be perfectly happy to sit with you and counsel you on your life's problems. I'd even be glad to meet you four times a week for in-depth psychoanalysis. And no, we don't need to have sex at all.

Sometimes I can tell that I've just given a trick the time of his life, and even had a great time while doing it. For some reason, these are the clients who never call back. Maybe I've given them too much pleasure; maybe I should have left something to be desired. Or maybe the trick is just afraid. In any case, if you have fun – please call again!

Remember that I am not a machine. I cannot lie down on the bed and let you fuck me like a blow-up doll, though I'd be happy to advise you on where to purchase such a doll. Similarly, I cannot get hard at will and fuck you for sixteen hours while you do rails of tina, though I'd be happy to advise you on where to get a dildo, or even a fucking machine. Sex with a whore is still sex with a human being – usually someone more exciting, brilliant, and experienced than usual – and we still need to negotiate the specifics of our interaction, arousal and pleasure.

When I say that no, I don't party, that means no. I don't want to do "just a little," "a bump," "only a hit," or a "booty bump."

Remember that this is a financial transaction. I'm here because you're paying me. Hopefully, we'll both have a great time in the process, but I am not going to fall in love with you... unless, of course, you show up at my house with a suitcase full of hundred dollar bills. But seriously: I used to have a regular client who paid me a substantial amount on a monthly basis. This was a great arrangement for both of us – it made me more financially stable, and it satisfied his need for a regular sex partner and a fun person to take out on the town. I made it very clear, from the beginning, that though I enjoyed this client's company I would not be spending time with him if it weren't for the financial arrangement. Nevertheless, after several months it all came to a head when the client "realized" that I was not going to fall in love with him, even though I had told him that at the very beginning. It was a disaster.

And finally, remember: Sex is supposed to be fun. We don't have to take this too seriously. It's okay to laugh, to talk like human beings and not just grunt machines or porn soundtracks, and to experience whatever intimacy or pleasure arises in our short time together.

Some of the Best Clients

by Veronica Monet

How do I define an excellent client? There isn't just one single description. I have had some of the best clients imaginable, and I've marveled at their variety. But if I had to choose one quality that would define a great client, it would be integrity.

> \In*teg"ri*ty\, n. [L. integritas: cf. F.
> int['e]grit['e]. See {Integer}, and cf. {Entirety}.]
> 1. The state or quality of being entire or complete; wholeness; entireness.
> 2. Moral soundness; honesty; freedom from corrupting influence or motive.
> 3. Unimpaired, unadulterated, or genuine state; entire correspondence with an original condition; purity.

A person with integrity does not play games or delight in manipulation. A person with integrity puts their cards on the table and derives joy from sharing from their heart, and they usually enjoy learning more about you as well. Their happiness is a shared happiness, never obtained at the expense of another.

My best clients have been honest and generous, not only with their money but with their essence. They have jumped at the opportunity to show their inner selves and to peer into me. They have approached life and pleasure as an activity which always has a spiritual dimension. They have learned to abandon themselves to spontaneous moments of joy and mutual bonding. They are able to let go of expectations and control long enough to realize the miracle of each moment. Perhaps experience has taught them that happiness and orgasms are not to be forced, but welcomed.

Early in my career as a courtesan, I thought "stuff" made for a good client. The more money he spent and the more he pampered me, the better I rated him. But experience has taught me that the truly great clients need not be wealthy. Granted, first-class travel, five-star restaurants, Broadway plays, shopping sprees, expensive birthday gifts, huge tips, and hot rock massages are not to be taken lightly. But the intent and emotions behind these extravagances are more important than the amount of money spent.

Therefore, I put the luxurious two-day trip to New York that nets me $16,000 right alongside the one-and-a-half hour outcall appointment for $500. Obviously, my bank account doesn't see the similarities, and since I value money, I can't help but assess the appointments differently when it comes to economics. But my feelings about the clients have little to do with the amount of money they spend, and everything to do with the energy they bring to our time together. The little things really do make a difference, and heartfelt effort never goes unnoticed.

For instance: I was recently greeted by a client with a room filled with incense and meditative music. Goddess figurines abounded, and my eyes were drawn to a simple altar. There, my fee was sandwiched between several CDs. These were not just any CDs: they were the musical creations of my host, and as such they were deeply personal gifts coming from his core. He creates spiritual music and his spiritual path is heavy with goddess influence. Consequently, the hour and a half that we shared was like one long prayer, and I was honored to serve as a conduit for the Great Goddess. I left full of joy, peace, and wholeness. Potent sessions like these transcend the one-dimensional definitions of job or money. Of course the money is important. But when I think of this client, I don't think about how much money he gave me. I feel a warm glow in my heart for him, and I feel validated in my professional calling as a sacred prostitute.

I find life is happiest when I remain open to it. So I don't establish a specific set of criteria that clients must live up to in order to be special. They are special if they approach me with integrity. Integrity requires that your soul get naked, not just your body. I have been transformed by my clients because of their vulnerability and honesty: my life is richer because of them, and my heart is fuller. Vulnerability, honesty, integrity: they look different on each individual. But it is always a special thing.

Last week, I walked through a client's garden. We marveled over the tomatoes and sweet peas. I bit into a fresh pea pod and quickly devoured the whole thing. Nothing is more decadent or delicious than eating vegetables off the vine. He gathered some summer squash and peppers for me to take home with me. Now every time I peer into my vegetable crisper, I am fondly reminded of that innocent moment in his garden, as well as the tender hugs he gave me while we were together.

It's an old cliché, but I've found it to be true: "it's the thought that counts." It really does not matter whether one spends a fortune or nothing at all. The only thing that really matters is one's intention. I have had men double my fee in an attempt to impress me, or perhaps to feel some sense of power over me. That is money earned the hard way – there's no real connection, just posturing that leaves both people feeling empty. I would much rather a client invest his being, let go enough to truly enjoy himself, and take some pleasure in my happiness. Sure, the cash comes in handy – but it's small payment for a lousy memory.

Conversely, the fact that something is very expensive doesn't diminish its value as a heartfelt gesture. I have had some absolutely magical dates that were incredibly expensive. A wealthy man can be just as sincere as a poor man. And some poor men can be just as egotistical and shallow as some rich men. If there is one thing I have learned about men over the last decade, it's that what's in his pocketbook will tell you very little about what is in his heart.

I love flying to a new city to meet with a client over dinner, and perhaps attend the symphony or theater. I love strolling along a moonlit pier or making out in a limo. I love wearing expensive clothes and eating the best food money can buy. I delight in a work schedule that accommodates time for a workout and massage, and perhaps a stop to shop for designer couture. But what makes this type of date attractive to me (aside from the hefty fee) is the personality and values of the client. I simply will not endure the company of a man who is overbearing or domineering or shallow. This is especially important when you're spending extended time with someone. The more time you spend together, the harder it is to pretend you enjoy their company; and if you're not having a good time, neither will your client. Both people must enjoy themselves or the date is a bust – whether you're dating for a fee or for free.

If I'm genuinely enjoying myself, there's no need to fake my enthusiasm. Earlier in my career, I did quite a bit of acting and enduring – for a much lower fee, I might add. Now I've become so accustomed to true joy in my work that I have no stomach for acting. It's interesting how, as your self-esteem grows, life responds by bringing you what you believe you're worth. So as I've raised my rates and insisted on enjoying my work, I've become better at what I do – and attracted a much better clientele.

Of course my ideal client is not defined by his profession, his bank account, or his appearance. He (or she – I've had about half a dozen female clients who came to me on their own, but most of my female customers have been accompanied by a husband or boyfriend) is someone with integrity and sincerity. Someone who is open to experiencing a spiritual dimension to their sexuality, or at least an emotional component to their physical gratification. I have nothing against fucking: I just got bored with it. And I refuse to do anything I find boring. Fortunately, there are so many intriguing and delightful people on this planet that it's really unnecessary to waste time with those who are not.

I guess this all has something to do with my own integrity. It has become increasingly important to me to experience a wholeness and honesty with my work. I don't care very much what labels are ascribed to what I do. Whether I am called a courtesan or prostitute or escort or whore, I am intent on achieving a particular aim with my chosen profession. I take great pride and derive immense satisfaction when I can bring a moment of clarity or a sexual healing to my clients. I would no sooner do my job for free than anyone else would or could. Even priests insist on getting paid. But I do what I love and the money follows. This concept works in all things, even sex for money.

And the best clients understand the importance of sex to their spiritual life and vice versa. They may not be able to express their intuitive feelings, but some part of them wants to be free of shame, to welcome more pleasure into their life, and to connect with another person both emotionally as well as physically. Some part of them craves the wholeness of integrating their sexuality with the rest of their life.

Dear John: There're Some Things You Ought to Know About Us Shemales

by Joy James

What do you want? Please tell me exactly. That's all I ask.

Honesty might seem like a silly, even puzzling, request coming from a T-girl like me. An honest shemale? Surely that's a contradiction in terms, just like my body itself – a sexy woman every place except where it counts the most, the gender-defining genitals between my legs. An honest shemale – when my whole life is a bit of a lie? And I have to admit, a pretty big lie at that: to pass me on the street, you'd mistake me for a normal girl, but tucked in my panties is my little secret. (Oh, how I wish it were littler.)

But it is not my intention to deceive, to be an artificial lure. You have to believe me. All I want is what any girl wants: to be accepted as a normal and natural (not to mention beautiful) woman. So if I walk like a girl, talk like a girl, and you want to fuck me like a girl, you must understand that it's hard and frustrating for me to interrupt things – to stop kissing you and push you away and say, "Honey, there's something you ought to know before we go any further."

Now, if all I ended up doing was giving you a BJ, it wouldn't matter, would it? You'd never know the truth. All you'd know for sure was that you had just received the best oral sex any girl had ever allowed you to experience. At which point you couldn't handle the truth. You might hit me – or worse.

So it pays to be honest. And now whenever I'm with a guy, I don't pretend to be anything other than what I am: a male-to-female pre-op transsexual, or shemale. Anyway, there're apparently lots of guys out there – judging from my many clients – who prefer me that way. Not real but a make-believe girl.

By the same token, the clients – you! – should be honest with me. The sex will be so much better. Trust me. I know. You want to get your money's worth, don't you? Then tell me well beforehand, when we're talking on the phone arranging "the date," what you want me to do. Exactly. The more graphic details, the better. Don't be embarrassed. I want to please you. It's good for business – for my clients to be happy and satisfied. That makes me happy.

There's a delicate balance between clarity and discretion, of course, and most escorts are wary of getting too explicit on the phone beforehand. After all, you might be a big, bad cop! But since I never talk directly about money (for new clients, my escort service handles all the crass commercialism), I believe it would be hard to entrap me for soliciting. So I don't worry my pretty head about it, and I can just focus on giving you head!

I'll do just about anything, if the price is right. But I can do without sudden surprises. Then I might not do what you want. Then neither of us will be happy. What do you want exactly? Please tell me. All I want is to please you. So, please, you must be honest. It'll be fun, this foreplay, just like phone sex.

Anal sex? Then you'll have to wear a rubber. If you insist on bareback, then we'll have to call off the date. But I have some specially lubricated condoms. You won't even know the difference.

I'd love to suck your cock. That's my specialty. But if you want me to swallow, you'll have to bring proof that you're disease-free. I love the taste, but not the after-taste if it's laden with germs.

Want to make me your bukkake babe and shoot all over my face? While there's nothing I like better than a cum facial, it really hurts when it gets in my eyes. So I'll wear my glasses. You don't mind, do you? Cum on my glasses is really a turn-on for most men, but if you don't make passes at girls who wear glasses, then maybe I'm not the girl for you.

Threesomes or more, BDSM, water sports? Whatever. I can get into that. But every girl has her limits. So if I'm not comfortable with what you propose, I promise I won't hang up. Instead, I can probably recommend a girlfriend who's "special" just like me. I don't want to disappoint you. If I can't please you, then I bet I know someone who can.

Now comes the fun part. What do you want to do with my big clit? I mean, dick (gigglegiggle). That's why you called me, right? You saw my web page or were referred through my escort agency. "A chick with a dick... an incredibly sexy babe with that something extra... 38C-28-38, plus 6 inches, cut...." That's me, the way my escort service advertises, quantifies, and objectifies me.

To you, that "something extra" must be a turn-on. Otherwise, you wouldn't be calling, right? But now that we're being totally honest, there is something you should understand. Although for you it's a turn-on, for me it's a deformity.

Think about it. The girl-with-a-cock of your dreams is not exactly what I – or most T-girls – had in mind when we started altering our bodies. If we were happy with our cocks, why in the world would we go through the expense and pain of trying to become women? While genetic girls (GG's) may love to be loved for their imperfect selves – plump or skinny, naturally blonde or happily highlighted, short legs or tiny breasts, warts and all – there's a problem when the wart is a penis.

Like any normal male-to-female transsexual, all I really want is wart-removal surgery. And that's why I took up escorting – simply to pay my bills for the never-ending electrolysis, collagen injections, and estrogen therapies, not to mention breast augmentation, cheek implants, browbone reduction, and Adam's apple shave. Plus I need to save enough for the cash-up-front sex-change operation itself – to fashion a facsimile cunt.

That's probably not what you want to hear. Your fantasy, like that of most T-girl-loving heterosexual males, is that we shemales are supremely oversexed, exotic creatures who love to fuck anything in sight. I've learned to play to that fantasy. But it's not easy. I have to prepare. You see, my penis is atrophied to the point of perpetual limpness after years of girlie hormone therapy. So in order to be "fully functional," I take Viagra fifteen minutes before I meet you. I bet you didn't know that, did you? From all the porno pictures of us shemales, you'd reasonably think the exact opposite: that our big clits – I mean, cocks – are in a state of permanent hardness, just waiting, willing, and wanting to ream you.

So, yes, I can be your "top." But in the interest of full disclosure you should understand that, for me, it's not very different from a genetic girl with a strap-on. Of course, I don't pretend to speak for all T-girls. Transvestites or crossdressers, for example, are just that: they dress up like girls. Their cocks get hard just pulling on their panties. Maybe that's what you really want, instead of an estrogen-altered transsexual like me? A TV, unlike a TS, can give you a mouthful or assful of cum with no problem.

But if you treat me like the anatomically correct doll I was meant to be – who knows? – maybe I'll even have an orgasm, too. Then I might give you a discount! That's right. So let me drop on my knees to service you. Or let me lie on the bed with my head tilted over the side, so you can pump me as deep as you want. Trust me, it'll feel just like a cunt. If you let me leave my panties on, you'll never even see my big clit and I won't have to blush. So you can then hump me, even pull my panties aside to fuck me while using my specially designed vibrator on my big clittie. I'll cum for you, I bet.

Hope you don't mind my being so totally candid, sweetie. And you don't mind my calling you "sweetie," do you? For I know the name you gave me over the phone wasn't real. That's okay. But if everything else is honest and true, we'll have a great time, I promise. Confide in me. Make me not only your special lover but also your special friend. Even telling me you're married is a good thing to know. You wouldn't believe what a turn-on it is for chicks with dicks, like me, to realize that you'd rather be with us than the real pussy waiting for you back home.

Samuel

by Annie Sprinkle

When prostitution is good, it's great. For example, with my favorite client, Samuel. We have a perfect relationship.

Samuel is my favorite trick. I've been seeing him for seventeen years now, and we're still going strong.

We first met when I was shopping, eyeing a smokey topaz ring in one of those jewelry/camera/souvenir stores on West Thirty-Fourth Street. He was in his fifties and the owner of the shop. I was nineteen, and had just moved to New York City. We flirted heavily, and eventually decided to make our transaction a barter – one smokey topaz ring in exchange for one blowjob in his office (it seemed like a decent deal at the time, but I later found out that the ring was worth only half a blowjob).

For several years, I shopped at Samuel's store. I got a camera, an enlarger, toaster oven, gold bracelet, and many other goods. He also introduced me to other great stores in the neighborhood where I could do barters with some of his friends and relatives.

Samuel was always the nicest and most respectful of all the guys I saw. As his business expanded, and he had less privacy in his office, I started to let him come to my apartment for cash. I rarely let tricks come to my home, but I liked and trusted him.

Samuel

Always super well-dressed in monogrammed shirts, expensive suits and ties, and fancy shoes, he looks like a million dollars. He has a full head of thick, white, wavy hair, and a muscular body from playing tennis four days a week. He is very Jewish, has a very hairy chest, and has a sweet smile. He grew up in an orphanage, never went to college, got married young, went into the camera business and did quite well for himself.

Samuel has helped me out in several emergencies. In 1981 he gave me some extra money for a deposit on an apartment I wanted. In 1984 when I was being audited by the I.R.S., he sent me his top accountant, whose pricey services I could take out in trade. He's given me sound advice on occasion, and always seems to call me just at those times when I really need the cash.

Sex with Samuel is always... pleasant, never a chore. To date, he's the best nipple sucker I've ever encountered, and the only person ever to give me nipple orgasms. He adores big breasts, which is possibly the main reason he's kept coming for seventeen years (pun intended). He's not interested in my pussy at all, or any sexual variety. Whenever I try anything the least bit out of the ordinary, he insists he's "just a meat and potatoes man." He doesn't want anything fancy, just a regular old BJ. I have to admit, it's nice not having to be creative to keep him coming back. I do try to make the blowjob last, though.

Samuel is one of those tricks that makes you proud to be a whore. He comes over-stressed and tense, and I can clearly see him relax and forget about all of his troubles for a whole hour. He tells me that I give him the most ecstatic, blissful, peaceful moments he ever has in his life on earth. He really deserves it, and he's very appreciative. With Samuel, I can take satisfaction in my work and talent.

My relationship with Samuel is by far the longest relationship I've had with a man. When we first met, he told me stories about his little children. Then came their high school graduations, their weddings, their grandchildren, then the divorces and their little drug problems. Once I passed one of his big stores on a summer's day, and I saw his son standing in the doorway. He looked just like Samuel, but half the age and even more handsome. I wanted to run up to him and give him a hug, say, "Hi! I'm Annie, I've known all about you since you were a little child. I've been your father's favorite whore for sixteen years now. Gee, I feel like we're related." But I held back.

Once, when he lost a bunch of money on the stock market, he asked me, "If I was broke, would you still see me?" I had to say something like, "You'll never be broke, so don't even think about it." The truth is that although I enjoy seeing him a lot, I know I wouldn't see him unless he paid me. We just don't have that much in common.

He's almost seventy years old now, and I do worry about him. He's had some heart trouble recently. Sometimes I think about how if Samuel died, no one would contact me to tell me. I might not know about it until two or three months later, as I never call him – he always calls me. I certainly wouldn't get invited to his funeral, even though I would really want to go. After all, we've been together for *seventeen* years. Just thinking about it gets me all choked up. If I died first, Samuel would certainly be welcome at my funeral, but I don't think he would want to be seen there. He's very secretive.

I sure wish there were more like Samuel, and I hope he keeps coming and coming and coming. Although he will never get to read this – he would get paranoid that I wrote about him and even used his real name – I would like to officially, publicly, sincerely acknowledge our relationship as a perfect relationship, mutually rewarding and satisfying, and give him my award for being *the best trick a girl ever had*.

I think I'll polish up that old smokey topaz ring.

Fall, 2003. Post Script:

I'm delighted to be included in this book. As I worked in prostitution for twenty years, it was a big chunk of my life, and I'm still very proud of my accomplishments there.

Samuel

When I moved away from Manhattan, I stopped seeing Samuel. He was my last client. (I'm glad the term "trick" isn't used much any more. When I wrote this story, it was what we called our clients.) Unfortunately, I lost touch with Samuel. I would have liked to stay in touch, to have a phone chat every so often, and see how he was doing. Maybe I'll Google him, and call and say hi, if he's still alive. I'd like that. And I know he'd love to hear from me, and would probably still want to see me!

Today I am quite a different person than when I saw Samuel. At the moment, I identify as a monogamous queer, an artist, Ph.D, author, mermaid, sexologist, and many more things. But if I had to choose my primary identity, it is still whore – although I am not a working prostitute, I am still very much a part of whore culture. Whores are my heroes.

I hope one day, whores will get more of the respect they deserve.

Paying For It

Strippers, Dancers, and Live Nude People

How to Talk to a Live Nude Girl

by Liberty N. Justice

"**P**rivate Pleasures," "Talk to a Live Nude Girl," "Fantasy Booth," "Encounter Booth" – they all mean the same basic thing: a one-on-one peepshow in which you can not only see a naked woman, but talk to her too. To the performers (who are usually peepshow dancers as well), it's a "talk-booth." For the customer, it's a place where the peepshow experience can be taken to a whole new level. (FYI, there are also talkbooths at male peepshows, but I know very little about them, so while much of my advice may apply there, the dynamic is probably at least somewhat different.)

I spent three years as a dancer and talkbooth performer at a peepshow in San Francisco. While dancing on stage with a bunch of beautiful naked women always had its pleasures, talkbooth was a mixed bag. Because the booth is interactive, the success of any one encounter depends on both the performer and the customer. A shift at an off hour could be a drag, but a nice busy lunch hour, with regular customers lined up for my show and happy to see me, was a pretty good time. At its very best, a "private pleasures" shift was entertaining, erotic, and fun, as well as lucrative, particularly when my customers put a little effort into making the experience a pleasure for us both. So in this chapter, I'll be offering you some advice on how to get the most for your money and time when you visit a talkbooth.

In case you don't know, a talkbooth is actually a small room divided in half by a large pane of glass, which is covered until the customer pays. Often the entertainer's side is decorated, mirrored and padded so she appears to be in a cozy box. The customer's side looks much the same as a viewing booth for a peepshow, with a place to sit, a mechanism for paying the fee and tips, and a sticky floor; there's also an intercom or telephone-like handsets so you and your performer can communicate.

The financial arrangements vary from place to place. Typically, the "support staff" (usually a guy at a front desk) can explain the payment system to you. Typically it involves a payment for time spent in the booth, plus tips for the performance. (Do not assume that the dancer is receiving the full amount of her "tips"; often the management is taking a share of both fee and tips.)

While there are some places where female customers are discouraged, women and couples were always welcome in the "Private Pleasures" booth where I worked. Most female talkbooth entertainers, lesbian, straight or bi, are delighted to see a female face – and body – on the other side of the glass. And if you and your partner are exhibitionists, an encounter booth is a safe, comfortable place for a couple to show off to an appreciative audience.

Many theaters have a number of encounter booths with a variety of girls ready to 4give you your own customized show. This allows the customers to pick a type of girl, or a girl they know and like. Some theaters, however, have only one or two booths, and thus a limited choice of entertainers at any given time. If there's a particular dancer you want to see, call ahead and find out when she'll be in the booth. When you do this, you are doing both yourself and the girl in question a favor, since there's nothing worse than trying to entertain a customer who's really wishing you were someone else.

Once you're in the booth, the quality of your experience depends on two things. One is the performer: her preferences, her mood, and her ability to negotiate. The other is your own ability to express yourself clearly and respectfully.

What always amazed me was how different all the dancers were in how they negotiated over what they would and wouldn't do, and for how much money. There were some girls who managed to solicit a tip in exchange for merely baring each exquisite portion of their body. An encounter with one of these girls is essentially a long slow tease, with anticipation being a big part of the fun. A girl like that often sees fewer customers, with each one spending a great deal of time and money for the privilege of spending time alone with her. Her customers tend to be wealthy regulars, particularly businessmen during the lunch hour.

I had the opposite approach in talkbooth. My customers were working-class men who appreciated a friendly girl who would get naked quickly and give them a good view of what they had come to see: large breasts, bare pussy, and a quick grin. I did charge tips for "special shows," which involved the use of toys – the cost increasing as the size increased. But most of my encounters followed my personal motto: "Get 'em in and get 'em off." The primary difference between seeing me in "Private Pleasures" and seeing me on the peepshow stage was that the talkbooth customer got all my attention, as well as the opportunity to see penetration, which wasn't allowed during a stage show. (This is often true of encounter booths: part of what you're paying for is the chance to see activities that aren't allowed on stage.)

If you know what you're looking for in a performer, you can probably find out whether or not a particular girl can meet your needs in a brief negotiation. If you're new to the talkbooth experience, try checking out a few different shows to get a sense of what's available. Since most encounter booth performers are also peepshow dancers, the stage show can give you a chance to preview the performers' looks and styles. If you like a certain dancer, ask the support staff when she will be in the talkbooth.

The other variable affecting your talkbooth fun is your ability to communicate with the girl in the booth. While many performers are quite empathetic, they aren't mind readers, so if you are looking for something in particular, you're going to have to tell the girl on the other side of the glass what that is. Keep in mind that complete candor isn't only to your benefit: the performer wants to give you a great show, so you'll tip well and come back often. The more information you give her, the better she can tailor the show to suit your desires.

What kind of information? Well, first of all, you can ask to see various activities. This is another difference between talkbooth and a peepshow stage: in talkbooth, it is somewhat more acceptable to "direct the show." This doesn't mean barking orders (unless that's the sort of show for which you have negotiated and tipped). It means saying things like "I'd like to see you play with your tits," or "Please hold your pussy open so I can see your clitoris," or "Could you jog in place and then touch your toes, like you're exercising." Some customers like to watch the dancer do something in particular to herself, such as slap her own butt or fingerfuck herself to orgasm. Other customers request more interactive activities from a performer, such as pretending to kiss or pretending to give the customer a blowjob.

Negotiating for the show you want will often involve tipping the dancer. If a performer has toys in her booth, feel free to ask what it would cost to see her use one or more of them. Other activities that typically require additional tips are dominance, submission or humiliation, any sort of anal action, or acting out a particular fantasy scenario such as "naughty schoolboy and strict teacher" or "teenager caught masturbating."

Don't, however, try to convince a dancer to do more than she has agreed to, or to give you more than you have paid for. This creates an atmosphere of conflict between the performer and the customer. It's impossible to get into showing off your body when you're being pressured to break your own limits. If what you are looking for is a struggle, negotiate for that fantasy – don't try to create it without the dancer's consent. And if the girl is having so much fun that she decides to give you a tiny bit more than you paid for, be grateful, and don't push it.

Of course, the biggest benefit to seeing a performer in an encounter booth instead of in a peepshow is that you can talk with the girl in the booth. And where you can talk, you can talk dirty. Go ahead and ask your entertainer the salacious questions you've been shy about asking other women. This is one lady who is used to being asked her favorite position or what an orgasm feels like to her. Trade a story or two, true or untrue, about the particularly wicked things you have done. Encourage the dancer to tell you how much she likes your penis, your nipples or your ass (or – if you are seeking humiliation – how woefully inadequate they are). And, of course, make sure to tell the entertainer how lovely and desirable she is.

What kind of language should you use in these interactions? Obviously, this being sex work, your performer is probably comfortable with any degree of explicitness or crudity. But there are some things I believe you shouldn't say to a talkbooth entertainer. Bothering her with repeated requests to meet her outside, or telling her that you're going to try to find her, is creepy and stress-inducing. (I myself was appalled when a customer, who had seen me on the news addressing a political issue, called me by my real name in talkbooth.) And threats of any kind, including stalking, assault, or rape, are completely inappropriate (except as part of a pre-negotiated fantasy) and should get you thrown out of the theater. Permanently.

Language, both positive and negative, involving the dancer's ethnicity (or other potentially controversial characteristics like religion, age, and body size) is a more delicate and ambiguous issue. I'm not naive about the degree to which many customers' fantasies and desires involve those aspects of a woman, particularly race; nor am I unaware of how performers incorporate those features into their self-promotion and shows. But I also know that African-American dancers get pretty sick of being told how black girls have great asses, and that Asian-American talkbooth girls have heard way too much about the charms of their petite, exotic, submissive selves. Even as a white girl I was annoyed when customers said they preferred white girls, and I got tired of being told by others that they "didn't usually like white girls." If race is an essential part of a pleasurable talkbooth experience for you, let your performer know this – and tip for it – before you start in with "baby got back" or "me love you long time."

Do feel free to compliment the other dancers at the theater. Your performer is probably perfectly happy to have a conversation about how hot one of the other girls is, and what you'd like to do with her. But please stay away from comparisons. Obviously, telling one dancer that some other dancer is prettier or sexier than her is not going to improve your show; there's not much that's erotic about a resentful or insecure performer, no matter how naked she is. And saying "Well, Sadie did it for only $5" is not going to convince her to drop her prices.

Less obviously, flattering one girl by insulting another girl is almost as bad. You may think "You have much better tits than Sadie" is a compliment, but for all you know, Sadie may be her friend – or her lover – and you may be turning your performer off by putting her friend down.

On the other hand, if there is something special you're looking for in a fantasy booth performer and you want help finding it, go ahead and ask. Just put it in positive terms. It never offended me to hear something like: "I have this thing for really tall, dark women. Is there a girl like that here?" It's not as if I don't know I'm short, redheaded and fair.

I did like to know what my customer was looking for, and a little of what was going on in his or her head. It's a little odd to be part of someone's fantasy when you have absolutely no idea what that fantasy is. For example, I was pretty freaked out by the guy who asked me to lie perfectly still on the floor of my booth. Sure, part of what disturbed me was the suspicion that he was pretending I was dead, but I would rather have known that than been lying there wondering.

However, you need to realize that for any fantasy, there is likely to be someone for whom that is the one thing they won't do. I only turned down one request for a specific fantasy in all the time I worked in the talkbooth: a man came in and wanted to hear me talk about beating up another woman in a fistfight. I just couldn't do it, and I told him so. I assume he found some other woman for whom it was no big deal, and that's fine. If your fantasy is that one no-no for a particular worker, ask another. You even stand a chance of finding an encounter booth performer who finds your fantasy as exciting as you do.

Do you doubt that for every customer fantasy there is at least one performer who loves it and at least one whom it squicks? I was convinced when I heard a former coworker talk about her least favorite talkbooth customer... and realized that she was talking about my favorite one! This was a man who went to talkbooths in search of an appreciative audience to whom he could show off his remarkable control of his anal sphincter, by doing what I referred to as "butt tricks" with elaborate toys he brought in. Far from being grossed out, I appreciated his willingness to entertain me.

This brings up a final important point: try to give something back to your performer. For most entertainers, the ideal "something" is money. Respect, courtesy, and a really big tip should be enough to make any talkbooth girl give you a great show. But if you can't afford to be a big spender, consider what you do have to offer. Give her a nice show, too, alone or with a partner; share an interesting fantasy or wild experience; or just encourage her to do whatever she likes to do while you watch and appreciate. And make sure you write her a great evaluation on your way out of the theater. All that effort can make up for a smaller tip. And don't forget to tell your stripper-loving friends to go check out her show, and say you sent them.

How to Find Your Inner Gentleman at the Gentleman's Club

by Jennifer Millis

Girls put up with a lot of shit working at a strip club. We're on our feet in stilettos for eight-hour shifts. We're normally cold for those eight hours, with outfits smaller than your average bathing suit, because management turns on the air conditioning to keep our nipples hard. We don't get health insurance. We don't have paid vacations. We don't have job security. We don't get an hourly wage. We work for tips alone. Depending on where we work, the club takes up to 50% of every dance, and often charges us a lofty stage fee of up to $240 per shift. Some of us work for Mafioso-style management that gives us the respect they might give an ant. And even though we're the cream of the crop in the sales world, we'll never be able to put it on our resume. Needless to say, when a girl is broke, cold, and cranky, with aching feet and a string up her ass, the last thing she needs is an asshole customer. So here's some tips on how not to be one.

HYGIENE AND GROOMING

Dancers spend heaps of time and cash looking good for their clients. Hair, face, body products, trips to the salon, waxing, manicures, pedicures, tanning, make-up, clothes, facials, and shoes are not cheap. All this makes us look fantasy-land perfect. We have the common courtesy to come to work with gum, mints, and mouthwash. And we have the common sense to come equipped with baby wipes and hand sanitizer, to make sure neither of us gets anything more than a lap dance. Some things you don't want to take home.

We like the same respect. One thing girls appreciate is a well-groomed customer. If you want us to get nice and close, then make yourself an appealing person to get close to. Basically, girls want to give dances to the sharpest-dressing, sweetest-smelling, best-groomed guy. Plus, you'll look like you have money – a sure bet on getting the most attention at a club.

Here are some specific pointers:

Take care of your breath. Chew gum, and use mouthwash or brush your teeth. The whole point of strip clubs is to get close to naked chicks. If you've been drinking, smoking, or eating stinky food, do something about it. Girls don't want to nuzzle their face next to yours or whisper naughty, naughty things in your ear if they can't stand your breath long enough to even ask you for a dance.

Shower. I can't believe I even need to say this, but shower before a big night on the town, and use deodorant.

Shave. Let's think about what happens at strip clubs. If you're lucky or have enough money, a girl will bury your face in her gazongas, smother you with her melons, or give you a good titty slappin'. Let's also remember how smooth stripper skin is. And smooth skin equals sensitive skin. No chick is gonna rub her soft-ass titties up against your hairy-ass face – so shave that five o'clock shadow! Plus, if you're a sucker for mommies or nurturing types, you'll get more face-petting on a smooth cheek than a bristly one.

Get manicures, either at home or at a salon. Every girl loves a hard-working man who can get dirty and lift heavy things, but not when your hands feel like gravel on our skin. And if you want to touch, which you all do, the following is a must. For any man who uses his hands at work (mechanics, construction workers, truck drivers, etc.), you must wash them and moisturize. Carry hand lotion and apply after a good scrubbing with soap and water. Get a manicure every week or every other week, especially if you are in any of the above occupations. Manicures cost a whopping 10-15 dollars at a salon. (And please, don't pretend you're too manly to set foot in a nail salon. You'll probably get more action there than at a bar buying girls drinks. Nail salons are full of women and only women; that means zero competition.)

Wear a clean, soft wardrobe. Have clean clothes on when you walk into a club. Girls are naked in a strip club. Sometimes when they are naked, they sit on your lap if you have enough money. And despite popular myth, girl tang is clean and surrounded by the most delicate skin. Most strippers are completely shaved, so there's not much protection between their jewels and your pants. If you come in with paint-encrusted carpenter's pants or layers of dirt, grease, sawdust, or chemicals, you're liable to give your favorite girl an infection. She'll miss work, she'll get shit from management – and she won't sit anywhere near you or your lap again. If you're coming straight from work with the guys, plan ahead. Throw a clean pair of jeans in with your sack lunch before you leave for work in the morning. Change before you get to the club. And no wool pants. Ouch!

Remember that "Love Line" is full of shit. Recently on Live 105 Love Line, Adam and Dr. Drew have been giving advice on proper attire for strip clubs. They suggest wearing loose-fitting, thin-fabric sweats to get the most bang for your buck. But from a stripper's point of view, here are a few reasons why you might want to reconsider. First of all, if it's not the kind of gangsta sweatsuit Jay Z's sporting on MTV, you'll look like a shmuck. What dork wears sweats to a club? You'll scream desperate, creepy pervert with bad fashion, and are likely to be avoided or ignored. If you're lucky enough to get a dance wearing gear meant for the gym or sick days, you won't get much friction. And even if you're blingin' the most dialed suit, ladies don't want to feel your goods so up close and personal, and will normally back off on the grinding to avoid such unpleasantness. Strippers work at a gentleman's club, not an escort service. If you want something that intimate, save your tips and look up escorts in your local paper. And don't ever whip it out.

Safety. Because at some clubs dancers are completely nude, safety and protection are important. If you jiz easily, make sure to slip on a condom in the bathroom before your dance, especially if you insist on wearing flimsy pants. It's unsanitary and dangerous to wet your pants during a dance, especially if your dancer is fully nude. It is your responsibility.

GENERAL BEHAVIOR

Become a regular. The best way to get to know a stripper and to get her sweet on you is to become a regular. This means you come in once a week or once a month, to spend (hopefully) a hefty and regular amount of cash on your favorite girl and on her only. Other girls will know you're her regular, and she'll give you VIP status to stay that way. You'll get to know her schedule, you'll get priority over any other guy who walks in the club, and you'll generally get a better dance than she gives anyone else. Gifts are also appreciated, but only if they don't diminish the amount of cash you regularly give for the dance.

Keep your "dating" expectations reasonable. A lot of guys go into clubs expecting to take girls home, and I'll be honest – some girls do leave clubs with guys. But for those of us who don't, it's annoying when a guy continually pesters us for dates. And you're fooling yourself if you think a dancer will step foot out of the club with a customer without heaps of cash. So if she clearly says "no," don't press it; and if she seems like she might say "yes," be willing to drop a bundle. Otherwise, you're only inviting rejection and annoying the dancer, who has to continually turn down your advances. Furthermore, if she does say yes, be prepared to get nothing more out of it than dinner and drinks. Don't assume that you'll get laid because she's a stripper.

Always ask before you touch. Do not assume. Do not grope. Do not force, push, or pull at your dancer. Use your words. Use your manners. Use your inside voice. Be polite and develop communication skills. Treat your dancer like a person with boundaries, respect, feelings, good days and bad days. You'll get a better dance if the girl isn't worrying about policing your hands the whole time. Do not smack a girl on the ass as she walks by your chair. If you do, be prepared to be kicked out – or to pull out a twenty as she walks back to bitch you out.

Pay the naked therapist. Because girls work for tips alone, they can't be sitting around yapping hours away as you re-count your family history and wife or finance problems. If you want to talk, pay accordingly. There's nothing wrong with hand-ing a girl a twenty for sitting and talking with you for fifteen or twenty minutes. Dancers can make anywhere from fifty to a hundred dollars an hour on a good night. Therefore, you must pay accordingly for chat time. My favorite customer ever was a scientist who gave me a hundred bucks every half hour to listen to his genius theories on astronomy, poetry, and mathematics.

Respect the girls – all of them. Girls can get bitchy, which means strippers can get vicious; but despite the cattiness, a strip club promotes an environment for some serious girl bond-ing. There is unspoken etiquette between the girls that you boys will never know about, so don't try to fuck with a pride of lionesses who've been working together for months or years. It is in bad taste to talk shit about one dancer to another. And don't ever talk about one girl's beauty or lack thereof to an-other dancer (or anyone, for that matter). Every girl in that club is hard-working, and although we might not all love each other, we have a unique respect for one another. If you insult or critique one stripper to another stripper's face, you're ulti-mately insulting every stripper.

73

Know when to say when. When around ladies, it is important to monitor your drinking. Most people go to work to make money. Strippers are at work. They want your money. If you become too drunk, we will take all your money and you won't even remember the sexy dances in the morning. Know your limits or have a friend who will take care of you. Drunks can get aggressive. Do not yell at the girl on stage, or on the floor, or in a booth, to "take it off" or "show me your pussy." This is crude and not appreciated by the dancer or fellow customers trying to watch a sexy show and have a good time. Do not yell across the floor for a girl. Get up out of your chair and approach her if you would like her services. However, most dancers avoid boozed-up jerks like genital warts. When you're three sheets to the wind, you might forget all your do's and don'ts and get your ass permanently 86'd.

The Fine Art of Tipping

Money makes the strip club go 'round. Tipping is the most important thing to understand about sex work. With the shady, power-tripping, sexist, money-hungry, high-on-blow managers taking a cut of every dance, girls rely solely on good tippers. If you want to even step foot into a club, you must have at least twenty dollars in your wallet. If you only have twenty dollars to spend, walk to the front row of the main stage, sit down, and spend three to five bucks on each dancer until you are out of cash. Once you've emptied your wallet, move away from the stage, sit a couple rows back and promptly tell any girl who approaches that you only had twenty bucks and you spent it all on the stage. Do not spend your twenty on a lap dance. You will be disappointed.

There's no such thing as a free lunch. If the minimum for a dance is twenty dollars and the club collects those twenty dollars from the dancer as a fee, then she's giving you a dance for free. Remember that you get what you pay for. In layman's terms, your dance will suck if the dancer doesn't get tipped. Don't waste twenty bucks on a lap dance that a stripper will probably refuse to give you. Instead, spend it on the stage, where you'll get more action, close-ups, and love from the girls. For those of you planning to get a dance, never walk into a club with less than sixty dollars. Sixty dollars will get you one really good dance. Of course you'll get a better dance for a hundred (and you must be prepared to spend at least eighty if you want to touch titties), but sixty is good bumpin' and grindin' butt-smacking fun.

And *if you have money to blow, blow it.* It's the most sure-fire way to make a stripper happy.

A FINAL WORD

Finally, remember that you are at a Gentleman's Club, so act like a gentleman. And don't forget, the more generous you are, the more generous we will be. Please turn off your cell phones and enjoy the show.

It's F5 Time

by Steve Mitchell
interviewed by Greta Christina

I've been working as a stripper for about ten years. I've worked for other agencies, but now I have my own business that I co-own with another guy. I perform at birthday parties, bachelorette parties, club shows... any occasion.

I classify my shows like they classify tornadoes: F1 through F5. I adopted this at a party about five years ago: I walked up to the door, and it looked like they were really screaming in there, and I said, "Okay, baby – it's F5 time." It means I'm just going to tear it up. I'm going to have a good time, I'm going to make noise, I'm going to scream and holler, I'm going to scare the living hell out of everybody – and they're going to have a good time.

When they're really into it, that's pleasant. When they're really excited, screaming, having a good time – but they're not too drunk – we like that. We feed off of the crowd. My energy is feeding off of you, and you're feeding off of me. Obviously in this business, money talks too. So if I walk into a party, and they're laughing and having a good time, and everybody's screaming and hollering, and there's money coming out, that makes it fun.

I did a party once for a 96-year-old lady who specifically requested a dancer in her nursing home. That was fun. It gave her a little bit of a thrill; she ordered it herself, and I got a big kick out of that. She was just smiling, hooked up to oxygen, having a good old time. And I loved it.

On the other hand, F1 is when I get to a party and it's completely off. They're totally not into it: nobody's doing anything, and they're looking at me like I'm a Martian. That's an F1. It makes me wonder, "Why did you even hire me?" And if the crowd is dead, I'm going to be dead. I still get the job done: I pour a little charm on, I crack a couple jokes. But I'm not as energetic.

One thing that annoys me about a party is when the people are belligerent. If they're too drunk, they get a little out of hand sometimes, and it's hard to control the situation. And there can be people I call "stripping hecklers." I don't get too many of them, but occasionally you get someone who's insecure or something, and she has to make comments about everything. That gets kind of annoying. If a party's going really badly, and the people are just being belligerently stupid, I actually cut the show short. I'll say, "Look, this isn't working out, and I don't feel comfortable being here."

I do parties for both guys and girls. I'm not gay, but I prefer gay parties. The gay guys seem to be a little more sophisticated when it comes to this business, and they treat me a little better. They're more appreciative, they tend to pay a bit more, and they're usually a lot more friendly. A lot of times, when a woman gets too drunk, she gets a little bit out of hand. I haven't seen that with gay men. They usually keep themselves under control. And I appreciate that.

I go to a lot of parties where they have good food, too. I always look forward to certain ethnic parties: Filipino parties, for example, are great, because they have good food. Little things like that are fun.

When the customers are organized, that makes it pleasant. When the person who books me has her stuff together –

she knows what she wants, she knows it's going to cost money, she knows they need to have tip money there, and she says that that's what they want and they're looking forward to seeing me – it makes my job a lot easier. It can be annoying if the customers can't make up their mind about what they want, and continually call me back time after time trying to figure it out.

I like parties where they book a week or two in advance. That's the best way to do it, because it gives everybody a chance to realize what's going on. I'm clear when I talk to the customer: I say, "Look, you're going to pay this amount of money, this is what goes on, it's a strip show, make sure you're prepared or the dancer will leave." When people call at the last minute, that's a red flag for most dancers. Nine times out of ten, it means nobody else knows the dancer is coming to the party. So when you get there, they're not prepared for you – nobody's brought any money, they don't know who the hell you are, and they look at you like you're some alien from a spaceship.

When a customer asks, "Can you bring down the price?" that's a red flag to me too. To be honest, I don't negotiate prices that much. I try to keep my price the way it is – I've been doing it a long time, and they're going to get a quality show. But a lot of the new agencies and the new people will bring their prices down. It annoys me when a customer calls up and says, "We called this other agency, and they offered this price." Well, if you want to go to them, go to them – but you're not going to get the quality.

Lack of information is a problem, too. When I talk to customers on the phone, a lot of times they tell me they're one age, and when I get there, they're not that age. Or there are men there, and they didn't tell me that. I'm asking questions, and they're answering my questions, but they're not giving me the entire truth. I've been doing this for so long that I can pretty much read any situation – and given their age, where they live, and what ethnicity they are, I can tell you how much money there's going to be at that party. If they're 18-year-olds, chances are they're not going to give me a whole lot of money; if they're older, my chances are better. So I need the information, so I can be prepared.

What customers need to realize is that we have the right to leave any time we want. The money we get to walk in the door is just that – money we get to walk in the door. Anything after that is tips. If you're not tipping, we're leaving. If they want me for an hour, and I get there and there's no tips involved, I'm not just going to stand around for an hour. Female dancers don't give a guy a lap dance if they're not getting paid. Female dancers don't go into a house party if the guys don't have any money on them. Yes, they get their show-up fee, but if they're not getting tips, they're not doing anything. They're going to leave. And we do the same thing as the girls.

You'd be surprised what happens when a male dancer walks into a show. A lot of people walk around with a closed mind, and they want to have these so-called "morals." But when you walk into a show, those same people will be the ones jumping all over you. It's a very hypocritical society. When I tell people that I'm a dancer, some of them snub their noses, and others say, "Oh, that's fascinating." I guarantee that at a party, the people who snub their noses will be all over me. It's so funny.

But when I go to a nice house, and they've got the money, and they've got good food out, and they're screaming and hollering, and everybody's happy, and they're asking me questions about how I got into the business… those parties are nice. And most of the parties are like that. Very seldom do I have parties that are disturbing. They're usually pleasant. And the more they're laughing and having a good time, the more pleasant it is.

Private Dancing

by Ginger

I have worked as a professional stripper off and on since 1998. I first went to work at my local strip club to help pay for my wedding, and I went back a few years later to earn the down payment on our home. Since then, I've worked as a stripper at various private parties, as well as stage events.

I'm mostly here to talk about private dancing – bachelor parties, that sort of thing. But there are some common rules of courtesy that apply to all stripper customers – in clubs as well as at private shows and parties. Let's get to those first.

First of all, not every stripper is a prostitute. I wasn't, and the dancers I personally knew weren't. I have no problem with that line of work, and I'm glad someone's doing it – no pun intended. But it's not what most dancers do, and we were – and still are – resentful of this assumption. Yes, I understand that some dancers will take money to perform sexual services. But don't just assume that you can offer me an extra $50 – or nothing at all, for that matter – and I'll blow you. Tipping generously does not entitle you to sexual privileges. If you want to pay someone for a blow job, that's fine – but it's not what I'm there for. Please don't assume that it is.

Second, at least in the states where I worked, a "no touching" rule was strictly enforced. I sure as hell was enforcing it. I once had a drunken elderly man ask if he could smack my ass while I danced in front of him. I politely smiled and said no, that paying to touch was against the law. He then asked if he could just stick his tongue in my asshole. "What part of 'no touching' do you not understand?" I asked him. He just grinned and reached out for me. Realizing that this particular location didn't have a bodyguard to help me, I grabbed my gear and left the building. So respect my personal space. I will touch you if I'm comfortable with you – and if I want you to touch me, I'll tell you.

This begs the question: what makes me comfortable? Simply being polite goes a long way. Smile. Be friendly but not touchy-feely friendly. And be clean. Seriously! Take a shower, brush your teeth and wear clean clothes. Aftershave or cologne is a nice touch, but don't put on so much that it enters the room before you do. I generally avoid having any contact with, or paying prolonged attention to, patrons who are filthy, reeking of B.O. or patchouli, have bad breath, or have the smell of day-old alcohol oozing from their pores. I take a lot of time to be presentable, clean, and nice to smell. I think it's only fair to ask the same of my clients.

Alcohol use is another big warning sign for me and other dancers. (See the above story for reference.) My guard is up the instant I can tell you've been drinking. Drunk men and women tend to be grabby and invasive, and I tend to avoid them. It's no big secret that alcohol impairs your judgment. A couple of beers may convince you that I'm really for sale, or that grabbing my breasts is a really good idea. Sorry, but no amount of alcohol is going to make either of those things happen. I don't want you passing out halfway through a dance, and I sure as hell don't want you vomiting on me (I've seen it happen and it's not pretty). I want your total attention and all of your judgment intact, thank you very much.

Being a good customer has its rewards. When I was working at the club, I had a good client who bought quite a few private dances from me. He was a total gentleman, never asked for anything, and was actually one of the nicest, most generous people I've ever met. And he was really into my persona. Through our many conversations, I learned he was a firefighter and that he loved his work. I liked him so well, I bought a vinyl firefighter ensemble that I'd only wear when he came to the club. He was very appreciative!

These guidelines apply to pretty much all strippers, no matter where they work. But there are some additional things that apply to the special circumstances of private shows, such as bachelor parties and the like.

First, be prepared to pay a hefty sum to get me to your location. I'm not saying it'll cost you thousands of bucks, but taking me or any other dancer out of the relative safety of a club demands a fair and elevated price. I probably haven't been to your neck of the woods or that particular hotel room – it's going to be foreign to me. I'm going to be in a place where I don't immediately know where the exit doors are, or even where the bathroom is. Obviously I'll find all that when I get there, but there's a definite personal risk involved, not to mention gas money. Hence, you'll pay more to have me there – and you'd best tip as well. And don't expect extra time for no extra money. This is my job, and I need to be paid for my time. The better the money, the longer I'll stay – provided I feel safe.

Oh – and I will arrive with an escort. In other words, a personal bodyguard, someone who's there to make sure I am not harmed in any way. It might not be you I'm worried about – you're reading this book, you know the rules – but the guy sitting next to you at your buddy's stag party may have different ideas about my role in the event. Be nice to the escort/bodyguard: he or she will generally respond in kind, and a happy, comfortable escort equals a happy, comfortable dancer.

The best thing you can do to ensure a good time for your private show is to plan things out ahead of time. Find a dancer you like at your local club, ideally someone you're a regular with, and ask if she does private parties. Most clubs insist you book the dancer through the club directly – but then you end up paying both the club and the dancer. Many dancers will barter with you personally, but they'll do so under the risk of reprimand from the club. For best results, be discreet. (You can generally find private dancers in the Yellow Pages as well – but be aware that you're shopping blind when you do that, and you won't know what their work is like.)

Once you've found your girl, negotiate what she's willing to do. You may hope to God that the stripper at your co-worker's bachelor party will do that trick you saw at another party – you know, the one with the whipped cream and the cherries? But you can't just hope for that. You gotta ask up front what your performer is willing to do. Otherwise you'll feel cheated, she'll get shortchanged in the tips department, and no one goes home happy.

Personally, I usually make a lot more physical contact with clients in a private show than I do in a club – if I'm not at a club, I don't have to follow their rules. But that doesn't mean I'm going to have sex with you. I'm a stripper, not a prostitute, remember? If you want a prostitute for your party, that's fine. Hire one.

Make sure the venue is clean. If there's filth everywhere, I will leave the minute my time is up. Having a bathroom handy is key as well, especially if there's costume changes involved. And the weirder the location, the higher the price. I'll show up to your bachelor party bonfire on the beach, but you'd better believe you'll pay top dollar to get me there.

Finally, be careful what you wish upon the groom at a bachelor party – you never know what will come back to haunt you. I did a party where I was paid to humiliate the groom-to-be. I strapped him to a toilet in the middle of the room, stripped him of his shirt, and had the men at the bachelor party pay me to whip him with my riding crop. He loved every minute of it and so did the party-goers. When I was finished with him, he immediately reached for his wallet and dumped the contents in front of me. He handed me a huge wad of cash and said, "Now it's their turn!" He had me return the favor – lash for lash– to each of the men who had paid for his beatings. I was happy to oblige.

While a lot of what I've said may make me sound like a frigid bitch, that's not entirely the case. My professional presence may be harsh (the role of bitch/dominatrix comes easily to me), but I am far from frigid with most clients. I can get quite physical when I lap dance. I'll sit right down and grind – when I'm comfortable. I'll make sure my vinyl boots rub your crotch ever so slightly – enough to scare you, but not enough to hurt anything. I'll breathe and moan into your ears, I'll lick and sometimes I'll bite – if you're good. My breasts will brush against your face, and my hoo-yah will be so close to your face you'll want to lick it – but you should know better than that.

It is, after all, a strip-tease. "Tease" being the key word. Don't forget that.

Greta's Guide
to the Peep Show

by Greta Christina

First of all – smile. Please don't just walk into the booth and stare at me like you're watching TV. I'm not a TV show, I'm not a porn video; I'm an actual living human being, dancing naked just a few feet in front of you. So show me that you're happy to see me. Leave the blank, couch-potato gaze at home in the TV room where it belongs, and give me a smile.

Look at my face now and then. Of course it's fine to stare at my tits and my ass and my pussy. That's what you're here for, after all. You want to look at naked women, without judgments or interruptions. And I have no problem with that; it's what I'm here for, too. But every once in a while, look at my face as well. Make eye contact. Smile. You'll get a better show from me; partly because I'll like you better, partly because I'll be able to read you better, and partly because I do really sexy things with my eyes and my lips and my face, and I can give you a much hotter show if you don't ignore them. So look at them. Show me that you know I'm really here; heck, show me that you know *you're* really here. Give me a little wave, or say hi, or something. And then go back to staring at my tits if that's what you feel like doing.

Talk to me, baby, talk to me. Ask me my name; tell me your name; share your searingly perceptive opinions about Wittgenstein if you like. You certainly don't have to make extensive conversation; I understand if you're feeling shy or aren't good with words or just don't feel like talking. But a simple "Hello" and a few words are a nice acknowledgment that I'm a human being, and I'm much sexier when I feel human than when I feel like a robot with boobs. If you're awkward and tongue-tied and don't know what to say... well, compliments never hurt. Of course I know I'm pretty and hot – I'm getting paid to be looked at, for heaven's sake – but it's good to hear it anyway. Be specific if you like: say that I have nice breasts, pretty hair, sexy feet, enticingly dimpled knees. And if you compliment me on something other than my body, you'll get major bonus points. Say that you like my outfit, my dancing, my tattoos, my searingly perceptive opinions on Wittgenstein, anything. Whatever it takes to open your mouth. (One thing to keep in mind, though: In the place where I worked, I was dancing right under a very loud sound system, and while the customers could hear me okay, I couldn't hear them for shit unless they shouted. So a complex and carefully worded debate about Wittgenstein may not be an option. If you're going to a peep show with loud music and you want to actually converse with a dancer instead of just shouting a few words, you might do what one of my favorite customers did: Bring a notebook and pen, write what you want to say, and hold it up to the glass.)

I know I said to just open your yap and say something, anything. That isn't exactly what I meant; there are definitely things you shouldn't say. Some of these are glaringly obvious, and I'd love to assume that nobody in the world would say them to a strange woman they're paying to look at naked, except that bitter and annoying experience has taught me otherwise. So here's the duh list: don't insult me, don't criticize me, don't curse at me or call me names. Duh. And for God's sake, don't put me down for being a stripper. I mean, double duh. But there are some other no-no's that are less obvious. For one, when it comes to those compliments, you might stay away from coarse language. I know that seems silly; I dance naked for a living and it's not like I'm going to faint dead away at the sound of a few salty words. But I still find it more pleasant to hear "You have beautiful breasts" than "Nice tits, baby." Especially from a stranger. Crude language is just ducky with a lover who loves it, but it can be a bit jarring from someone I just met. It's not a huge deal, it's certainly not the most important piece of advice I have to offer, but it's something you might want to think about.

Much more importantly, I hate being ordered around and told what to do, and so does every dancer I've ever worked with. So please don't do that. Don't beckon me to come closer, don't tell me to spread my pussy, don't tell me to turn around and show you my ass. Let me run my own show. If I like you, I'll get around to asking you what you'd like, and then you can tell me. Now, if there's something you're just dying to see and it's going to completely ruin your day if you don't see it, then sure, go ahead and ask for it. But do ask for it – don't demand it. And ask nicely: say "please," and be prepared to accept "no" for an answer, without arguing or sulking. Don't boss me around. You want a professional submissive, excellent. You have my blessings. That's a perfectly reasonable thing to want. Go for it. And go pay for it. To be brutally frank, you're paying for my time in quarters, and that's not nearly enough money to earn my submission.

But in all honesty, the words from a customer that freaked me out the most weren't "Show me your pussy" or even "Show me your pussy, bitch." The words from a customer that freaked me out the most were "I love you." That was deeply weird and disturbing. To this day, I have no idea what was going on in that guy's head. I mean, he had just met me thirty seconds ago, and I use the word "met" extremely loosely. Did he really think he loved me? Was he acting out some fantasy of being in love? Did he think that this was the way to get a girl to be nice to you? What the fuck was he thinking? And what did he expect me to do? Was it okay for me to just smile and say "Thanks"? Did he expect me to say "I love you" back? Did he think I was going to run off the stage and into the sunset with him? Christ, did I have to worry about this guy turning into a stalker? I felt awkward and scared and totally put on the spot. It was the only time at that job that I was completely at a loss about what to say or do. So what I wound up saying was nothing, and what I wound up doing was smiling weakly and getting the hell away from that window as soon as I gracefully could. Not good. No fun for either of us. Don't do it.

Creepy guys who think they love their strippers notwithstanding, you may have noticed a pattern to my advice. Give me a smile; give me a greeting; give me a compliment or a little conversation. Give me a kiss, even: I know there's a pane of glass between us and we can't really kiss, but pretending to kiss through the glass is sweet and fun and a refreshing change of pace, and it's one of my favorite things to do. Flirt with me; give me a wink, a coy sidelong glance, a waggle of your eyebrows. The guiding principle here is to give a little, something of yourself, something other than quarters. Don't just be a black hole, sucking up all the energy in your immediate vicinity. Bring something to share. You don't have to be fancy or witty or super-creative, but I can give you a better show if there's a little give-and-take between us. If you don't feel like talking much, maybe you could do something entertaining. Party tricks are often a good way to make friends: I still remember the young sailor who stood on his shoulders and sucked his own dick; the fifty-something businessman with the red lace bra and garter belt under his business suit; the hipster dude who came into the booth, took off his shirt, and danced for the dancers. These guys got great shows from me, if only because I wanted to keep them happy and entertained, so they'd stick around longer and keep *me* entertained. (We loved the last guy especially; he was a regular, and he got the best shows of anybody.)

But you don't have to make up a party trick just to show the strippers. If you happen to have a good party trick that you enjoy doing anyway, by all means, bring it to the show. But if you don't, a smile and a compliment will be plenty. If all you have to share is your appreciation... well, that's not insignificant. It's valuable, more valuable than all the party tricks in town. Show it.

And speaking of sharing, do bring your wife or girlfriend if you can, or even a female friend. More strippers than you might imagine are lesbian or bi, and even the ones who aren't often enjoy the variety of seeing a female face. At the place where I worked, the dancers would inevitably make a beeline to a window if we saw a woman in it. We'd jockey for position over who got to dance for the girl, and if it was slow, sometimes all four of us would dance for her at once. So going with a woman is a good way to make strippers happy and get them to pay attention to you. (If the woman wants to come, that is. Don't drag her in if she's freaked or dubious or just not interested. It won't be fun for anybody.)

Peep shows and other strip joints generally have house rules posted near the entrance. Read them. Learn them. Pay attention to them. It's no fun for me to have to play cop when I'm dancing, reminding you of the rules and trying to enforce them while I try to stay cheerful and pleasant and sexy. It puts me in an awkward position, and I don't appreciate it. And please don't come in drunk or stoned, either. It's not as bad for me as it is for flesh-on-flesh sex workers; at least I'm behind the glass and don't have to smell your breath. But getting bombed makes you stupid and sloppy, less likely to be charming and more likely to be obnoxious, and generally not very interesting to anyone who isn't also bombed.

If you're going to jerk off, bring something to jerk off into: a hanky, a tissue, something. We like the janitors who work here, some of them are our friends or even our lovers, and we hate it when their job is harder than it has to be. And for God's sake, don't squirt in the window. It's gross.

Finally, when you're about to leave, say thank you. We're more likely to remember you fondly if you do. Thanks for listening, and enjoy your show!

Dominants and Submissives

The Session: From Phone Call to Graceful Exit

by Mistress Simone Worthington

You've finally decided to call her – the professional mistress! All this time fantasizing, dreaming – now, if you can just dial the number. *Stop!*

THE PHONE CALL

Before you call, reread her ad. There are clues in it. What are her phone hours? Respect them. If they are 10 am to 2 pm, don't call at 9:45 and expect an answer, and don't leave a rude voicemail when you're disappointed. And don't call at 2:15 and expect her to spend the next hour chatting with you. These hours are posted for a reason. She may have a family, a job, or a session to go to.

Remember to address her as she's listed in her ad: Mistress Simone, Goddess Diva, Ma'am. Do not refer to her as "Simone," "Diva," or "Hey." Show the proper respect. If no title is given in the ad, choose a respectful prefix.

If she has a secretary, slave, or assistant who answers the phone, treat this person with respect as well. They obviously know why you're calling, they know the domina's procedures, and they can give you valuable information, such as the mistress's likes and dislikes. Do not demand to speak to the domina and only to her. You don't call your doctor and give her receptionist a hard time, do you? You'll probably be prompted with questions; they're geared towards finding out if you're a good potential slave for the domina, and they're meant to help both of you. Be polite and speak clearly.

Telling the domina your likes and dislikes will help make your session enjoyable for both of you. So before you call, have some idea about what type of fetish, training, and/or session you're interested in. This question should be asked early in the phone interview. And that's exactly what this call is – an interview. You must make a good impression if you wish to be granted a second interview.

Be honest at all times about your fetish experience. You don't want to tell a domina that you have experience with play piercing, and then pass out at the sight of the first needle. Likewise, don't say you enjoy heavy spanking if all you've had is a light over-the-knee. If you've never tried something, say so. Your honesty will be respected, and you may open some new doors.

Some questions you might want to ask are: Can I bring my own toys? What days and hours are sessions available? Inquire about what her specialties are. If you're into crossdressing, but the mistress isn't equipped to do this, you need to know. Ask about the equipment if you have a particular piece you need for your fetish, such as cages, suspension gear, or mummy bags. Not everyone has an entire houseful of dungeon equipment. And don't waste your time or hers if you don't want a session. Politely say "Thank you" and try someone else.

Asking for sexual gratification is not going to get you in the door. The prodom is not a prostitute. And you should not expect to see the domina if your only "fetish" is to worship her orally or anally. Don't hide behind words such as "servitude" or "worship." Skilled prodoms are becoming harder to find, so don't waste time asking for things she won't do. You can ask about release or masturbation if it's important to your scene. We're used to this question, it won't offend us.

Now the thousand dollar question – money. Yes, we have to mention it. Do not make this your first question. It is rude. Do not ask bluntly how much she charges, how much it costs, or what the price is. This will probably end the phone call quickly. Instead, always refer to the gift, token, or gratuity. Furthermore, do not go into sticker shock when a figure is mentioned. And if you have any money-related questions – are longer sessions available, are other dominants or submissives available, do different fetishes require different tokens – now is the time to ask them.

The last step is to schedule or not. If you want a session, now is the time to say so. If not, thank her for her time and end the call. If you're looking to schedule at a later date, say so and give some idea as to when. (This will prevent any disappointment when you call to schedule and she's out of town.) Make sure she has your name – or some name – so you won't have to repeat this whole process. If you are ready to make an appointment, have some flexibility in your schedule, and be prepared with a few options if your first choice is filled. At this time, you'll be given instructions on how to proceed to your next step – the actual session.

THE SESSION

Okay, you've actually done it! You've called the mistress and scheduled an appointment. The first thing to do is keep it! If for any reason you have to cancel it, or if you're running late, call and let her know. If you want a guarantee that you won't get to see her when you do call to re-schedule, be a no-show. It is rude and inconsiderate. Treat this like any other appointment – be on time!

You should also be clean, neatly dressed, and well-groomed. Be clean-shaven, wear clean, unstained clothes, have neat hair, and use deodorant. You will not have a satisfactory session if the mistress won't touch you because you smell. But don't go too far in the opposite direction and wear too much aftershave, hair gel, cologne, etc.

When you get to her location, the first thing to do is secure your car. Even if you're in a great neighborhood, take proper precautions. I can't tell you how upset a mistress will be if something happens to your car when you're at her place.

Enter the location quietly and discreetly. If you can't find the exact location, don't walk up and down the block asking her neighbors if they know where Mistress So-and-so's dungeon is. You could be putting her and yourself in danger. Every state has different laws about domination – so be careful.

Once in her waiting room, remember that you called her, not the other way around. Be respectful! Greet her with the title she uses. At this point, she will let you know what's expected of you (i.e., kneel, eyes down, sit, etc.). If there's a pre-interview, either at her location or a mutually agreed-upon place, the same rules apply. Do not enter her place like a storm-trooper, critiquing everything and bombarding her with questions right off the bat. Take a few minutes to let her assess you.

And take those same few minutes to assess her. Is she, in fact, the person whose picture you saw in the ad? Do the two of you click? Is the dungeon clean? Do you feel secure in the space? These are questions you should be asking yourself. Now is the time to bow out gracefully if your expectations are not met.

Speaking of your expectations, now is also the time to make your wants and fetishes known upfront. You should be respectful and non-demanding, but you must also be clear and honest. If you don't tell her that you like foot worship, and all you get is a spanking with no time at all at her lovely feet, you have no cause for anger. Don't go through the entire session unhappy and then grouch about it online afterwards.

Also, be patient. Everyone can have a bad day, and you may have come on hers! Most respectable dommes will communicate this fact to you. They will also ask if you have any questions before the "official" session starts. Do tell her if you have any health problems at all – it may affect your session, especially if you have bad knees or high blood pressure.

Once the session begins, the main thing to remember is this: If at any time at all you feel discomfort or pain (not the good kind), you must let her know. This applies to emotional discomfort as much as the physical type. She will have given you a "safeword" to use if you want the action to stop, and she should stop immediately if you use this word. If she doesn't give you one – ask for it. If she says she doesn't use them, think seriously about that before you go through with the session. How will you communicate to her if something is too intense? Does she care? If not, leave! I can tell when my slaves have had enough, even before they can, and once asked they usually admit it was time to switch activities. Don't be brave and take it for your mistress if it's too much for you. I respect an honest slave a lot more than a dead and dumb one.

If you follow these simple guidelines, both you and your mistress will have a much more enjoyable time together. You're there to experience your fetishes and you're entitled to a good session, but that doesn't entitle you to be an asshole. Be respectful at all times. Enjoy – this is what you were waiting for.

THE GRACEFUL EXIT

Wow! So that was your session! So many sensations, so many thoughts and emotions racing in your mind. Or maybe you feel like a pool of Jell-O. What to do now? Is she pleased? What hurts the most? Should you get dressed? Will she want to see you again? Will that leave a bruise? Did you really like that? *Stop!*

First things first – relax and take a few deep breaths. You just went through an incredible journey, and both your mind and body are reacting to it. Endorphins are traveling through your system, and your synapses are on full throttle.

Your mistress is still in control of the time, and will instruct you about what you should be doing now. Part of her skill is knowing what type of attention each submissive will need after a session. This is commonly referred to as aftercare. It can be anywhere from five minutes to half an hour, depending on the type of session, her style, and her schedule. But as a submissive, you want to pay attention to this seemingly small detail. Any experienced, knowledgeable Mistress will make sure you're all right after your session. If she needs your assistance in cleaning up, she will ask for it.

Keep in mind, however, that as a submissive, you are ultimately responsible for yourself. Mistresses are not mind readers. If you're feeling unwell after your session, let her know. Discomfort can be caused by any number of physical reasons: low fluids, high temperature, over-exertion, and so on. This is a key reason why, at the beginning of your session, you must tell the mistress about any health issues.

After an intense session, an uncomfortable silence can sometimes follow. Don't start jabbering. Remain politely respectful and ask if there is anything she desires. I always have my slaves get dressed, and then I sit and chat with them to get feedback. Feedback, both good and bad, is important to give. It gives her information to help make future sessions more fulfilling, and it helps her expand her skills as a professional. I've learned many new things from negative feedback. This doesn't mean you should give her a comprehensive list of what exactly was right and wrong with the session. Keep it simple. Your mind is still reeling and your endorphins are on overload. I encourage my slaves to contact me about 48 hours after their session, when they've had the chance to reflect on it with a clear mind.

Once you're dressed, keep in mind that your exit will still be under the mistress's authority. If she is pressed for time, she will usher you to her door and politely say her farewell. Every mistress says goodbye differently, so don't be offended if she appears curt or rushed. She may not have much prep time before her next session. Don't fall into friend mode unless she initiates it. Remain respectful, and above all – thank her! Even if it wasn't the best session you've had, be courteous. I like to close my sessions with a big hug, if I think the submissive will be comfortable with it; it lends a touch of humanity to a very intense encounter, and lets them know I really enjoyed our time together. Other mistresses will just boot your ass out the door. However the farewell is conducted, remember that a professional is just that – a pro. It is her job to help realize your fetish fantasy: if that has happened, consider it mission accomplished.

Congratulations! Now, go forth and session!

The Kinky Connoisseur: Tips and Techniques for Visiting Pro Dommes, Subs, and Switches

by Mistress Morgana

S o you've been harboring kinky fantasies, and you've decided to make an appointment with an SM professional to make them come true. Congratulations! While I've got an obvious bias (I've been a professional SM provider since 1995), there are many great reasons to seek out a pro. For starters, a good SM professional will have a high level of skill, ability, equipment, and aesthetic appeal. She'll provide a safe, sane, consensual, and judgment-free environment, where you can expect a high degree of discretion and confidence. The pro dungeon can be an emotionally hassle-free and safe space, without the responsibilities of personal relationships – and a visit to an SM pro can be a fun and kinky way to invigorate your love life and learn new fantasy skills with your partner. And most SM pros accept any client who is SSC (safe, sane and consensual) and willing to comply with their professional requirements – regardless of age, race, gender orientation, sexual orientation, looks, dis/ability, religion or ethnicity.

You'll notice that I say "a good SM professional." As in all industries, professional dominants, submissives or switches can vary in their skill level, experience, ethics, and commitment to client care. I'm writing this to help you navigate the tricky terrain of finding an SM professional, and to give you essential information that'll help you get what you want. I'm also writing specifically about women who do professional SM, since what men offer in this arena (especially to other men) can be quite different, and deserves a separate article.

Getting Started

Before you contact an SM professional, I highly recommend that you think seriously about the sort of experience – and the sort of person – you're looking for. If you're a new player, spend some time learning the language unique to BDSM. You can find how-to books and videos on BDSM at high-quality sex shops and online stores, or you can check out the websites of SM and sex information organizations (see the Resource Guide in the back of this book). Understanding the language, conduct and codes of BDSM will help you ask for what you want, and will make your visit to a pro more enjoyable.

Most experienced SM professionals – domme, sub or switch – have some sort of website, with detailed information about their interests and limits (as well as some delightful eye candy). Your best source is through advertising sites like the Eros Guide or the Max Fisch Domina Directory, which have links to SM professionals around the globe – both independents and members of a house. Independent SM pros are often more established in the community and thus tend to have higher fees. Women who work at a house may be newer to professional SM and often charge less – but that doesn't mean they're under-qualified. There's great value to be offered by both independents and houses.

It's important to note that many sex workers – from strippers to escorts – use BDSM or fetish imagery in their ads. If you're specifically looking for a pro domme, sub, or switch, look for ads and categories that are explicitly about BDSM. You'll notice that SM professionals often include the phrase "no sex" in their ads.

What's Up With "No Sex"?

Yes, of course – visiting a pro domme, sub or switch is meant to be hot and sexy. But the overwhelming majority of women who offer professional SM will not have any direct sexual contact with their clients. They aren't willing to take the legal risk, and in many cases they simply don't want to. So when you begin your search, you should understand that genital sex will not be a part of your scene.

Naturally, the definitions of "sex" can be subjective, and the boundaries between "sex" and "not sex" can be fuzzy. Some pros are happy to consider acts like strap-on play or golden showers (peeing on a partner), while others aren't. And many SM professionals will let you masturbate yourself at the end of the session – but they'll tell you upfront that they won't assist you in any way. If you're wondering what their policy is on a particular act, or if you're looking for something that falls into a "fuzzy" area with regard to sex, the best way to find out is to ask, politely but directly, during your initial phone call. Common acts that fall into the "fuzzy" arena are anal play, enemas, catheterization, body worship, golden or brown showers, "milking" (the use of hands-free sex toys to force orgasm), and giving fellatio to a dildo.

There are certain acts that SM pros will rarely consider, though, and you should assume that they're off-limits. Those acts include: any form of "pussy worship," which is really just a fancy term for oral sex; golden or brown showers given to a professional submissive; and any form of penetration done to a pro sub, vaginal or anal, including invasive medical scenes such as enemas or "exams" with a speculum.

The bottom line is that if you're looking for a directly sexual experience along with your kinky one (i.e., touching a woman's genitals, anus or breasts erotically, or having your genitals or anus touched erotically), your best bet is to find a kinky escort who enjoys using BDSM in her sessions. Search on-line ads or your local adult newspaper for a "fetish and fantasy" section, or simply browse the escort listings for women who advertise for kinky play. Or splurge on yourself – schedule time on the same day with a BDSM professional and a sex professional. Work yourself up in the dungeon, and then go visit the escort with all that sexy energy.

MAKING THE CALL

Once you know which professionals you'd like to speak with and what you'd like to do with them, your next step is a phone or email conversation. Most SM pros have regular phone hours when you can ask questions, discuss scheduling, and have a brief but detailed talk about your interests and level of experience. (If you're contacting a house, you'll probably speak with a secretary – not the woman you're scheduling time with.)

When you're contacting a pro domme or sub for the first time, the most important thing to remember is that we talk with hundreds of men (and women) every month. Some of these callers are chronic time wasters who call us instead of a phone sex service. Others are outright prank callers. Still others try to book and cancel appointments repeatedly, while pushing for detailed phone conversations. I've been told by many callers that they find SM professionals short or abrupt on the phone: if that happens to you, please remember that we field countless phone calls from people who are not serious or polite, and until you've proven yourself by scheduling an appointment and showing up for it, you may be asked to keep your calls and emails as brief as possible. (Having said that, you should expect her to treat you as politely as you're treating her.)

There are a few basic guidelines for setting up your appointment. First, before you call or email, make sure you've thoroughly reviewed her ad or website and are familiar with her interests and limits. I'm always amused by callers who claim to love my website – and then rattle off several interests that

I've clearly said are off-limits on my Frequently Asked Questions page.

Before you call, write out exactly what you're interested in, the dates and times that you're available, and the questions you'd like answered. You may get excited or nervous when you call, and your notes will help keep you from forgetting anything. Be sure to write down important information that the SM pro gives you, such as interests, limits, rates, and scheduling protocol.

If there's an activity or fetish that simply must happen for you to enjoy your scene, make sure you ask for it during your initial phone call. If thigh-high boots are central to your fantasy, or you want to give a submissive a very hard spanking, or it's important that you be allowed to masturbate at the end of your scene, let the woman you're speaking with know it upfront. Requests that aren't made upfront during the initial phone call won't necessarily be accommodated once you're in the dungeon.

Use your time on the phone to get a sense of who you're speaking with. SM is a highly personal exchange, and you'll find that every professional has her own style. Politely ask about her skill and experience, and trust your instincts. If she isn't right for you, don't book with her. If you book an appointment and then have second thoughts, respect her time by canceling with at least 24 hours' notice.

If you're a heterosexual couple calling for a couple's appointment, make sure you're both available to come to the phone. Men calling on behalf of their make-believe girlfriends or wives are common phone pranksters, and you'll make a good impression by calling as a couple.

Don't ask for a discount or barter arrangement unless the person you're contacting offers those options in her ad or website.

Finally, don't try to engage in SM fantasy role-play over the phone unless you're invited to do so. I enjoy kinky phone banter with people I've played with before, but most professionals won't even consider launching into a DS dynamic with a first-time caller. If you're a top calling a pro sub, it's especially important to understand that the role she plays in scene doesn't make her submissive to you 24/7. Phone hours are a time for a professional, polite exchange of information, and language you might find kinky or titillating can come across as rude or out of bounds to a woman who's simply trying to run her business.

VISITING YOUR FRIENDLY LOCAL DUNGEON

When you do make your appointment, the most important thing to remember is that you're scheduling professional time, and you should treat it with the same respect you'd give a doctor's appointment. Your domme or sub will probably give you very specific instructions on confirming your appointment and arriving at the dungeon. These instructions should be followed to the letter: they exist to protect your privacy as well as hers.

When you arrive for your session, be on time and well-groomed. Don't linger in front of the building or on the street corner. Never drop by without an appointment, and don't point out the address to your drinking buddies. I used to manage a B&D house, and occasionally I'd arrive early and wait in my car until my shift started. I would watch men pacing up and down the block looking anxiously over their shoulders, or skulking on the front step looking like they'd just committed a heinous crime, before finally "sneaking" up to ring the doorbell. It wasn't uncommon to see a man counting out his session fee in twenty-dollar bills as he walked up to the house. Another time, a client arrived at the door fully (and unconvincingly) cross-dressed in particularly slutty apparel, carrying a spreader bar with ankle cuffs. All this behavior is high-profile and highly suspicious. When you visit an SM pro, give her the same discretion that you'd like to receive.

Many SM professionals (particularly subs and switches) include pre-session negotiation in your appointment time. Negotiation offers you a neutral moment to establish safewords and review desires and boundaries, and it also gives you some time to "shift gears" from your daily life to your dungeon experience. Negotiation is also the time to tell your pro about any medical concerns you may have that could affect your session. A good SM professional will listen carefully to your interests and limits, and she'll expect you to do the same for her. Remember, every SM pro is different, and people's limits change, so don't assume that because you've done it before, you can do it again. I negotiate before almost every scene I do, even with people I've sessioned with for years. I enjoy having a moment to reconnect, and I like to check in about certain limits that can change from visit to visit. Most importantly, negotiation gives you a chance to ask direct questions and receive direct answers. A good SM professional won't be offended or shocked by a respectful request; she'll either be willing to do it or she won't, and she should politely let you know one way or the other.

EXCHANGING POWER AND EMPOWERING YOUR EXCHANGE

The exchange of power that happens in a professional SM scene can be confusing – especially when you're a submissive with a professional Mistress. On the one hand, you've made an appointment to experience loss of control and complete domination; on the other hand, you have specific fantasies that you're paying to have realized. Many clients are concerned about appearing bossy or "topping from the bottom." But there's nothing wrong with having a clear set of expectations. Just make sure you're visiting a mistress who's compatible with your interests, and be honest with yourself (and with her) about how much control you want – and how much you want to give up. When it comes to how much input and control you have in a session with a professional mistress, there are a few different options.

In all cases, you should expect a mistress to listen to and respect your general interests and your limits. If you schedule an appointment for an over-the-knee spanking in a strictly domestic setting and you can't take any marks, this is exactly the sort of session you should receive.

Providing a detailed list of your interests and limits can provide guidelines for your scene that can be very helpful to many mistresses. Such lists are not scripts or "to do" lists, and they allow the mistress to use her own creativity, expertise, and passions to drive the scene.

However, if you want a mistress to follow a formal script in which her speech or the things she does are dictated by your specific fantasy, you should politely state this upfront in your initial phone call – and be prepared to hear "no." Many mistresses feel that scripts rob them of their own unique input, and will not play with scripts of any kind. Others are happy to consider such scenes, as long as they match their own fetishes and interests. Your best chance of playing a scripted scene is to contact many mistresses, and find one who shares your fantasy and enjoys scripted role-play.

And if you're a masochist or fetishist who's not interested in power exchange or submission, you should find a mistress who's happy to give you the pain or stimulus you're looking for without needing to dominate you. I enjoy playing with masochists who are simply interested in pain; my only requirement is that they not try to top me into whipping them, or make me feel like I'm in service to their nipple torture. SM without power exchange isn't uncommon, but you should make sure during your initial phone call that the woman you're contacting is interested in that dynamic.

If you're a top contacting a professional submissive or switch, there's a whole different set of potentially confusing power dynamics. It's important to realize that your dominance has priority in the dungeon – but not on the phone or during negotiation. Negotiation and making appointments require neutrality, so the sub can explain her interests and limits, and if you try to verbally dominate her during this process, you'll only frustrate or annoy her. A professional submissive I trained once asked a client if he could move his appointment up one hour: he agreed, but said she'd be severely punished for her indiscretion. She didn't appreciate this play dynamic being pushed out of the dungeon and into her business procedure, and told him that she wouldn't see him at all. Threats of punishment and dominant language are awfully fun when you're playing, but you should respect the DS dynamic that a pro sub is trying to create for you in scene by treating her in a polite and business-like manner when you're not in the dungeon.

Similarly, when a professional submissive tells you her limits, she's not kidding around. Women who provide this experience are investing an incredible amount of trust in your scene, and if you don't respect that, you can expect to have your session cut short. Most pro subs come to their craft out of deep personal fantasies of submission, and this can make it especially frustrating when a client doesn't take special care to protect and respect their limits. It's good to remember that most pro subs and switches are considerably more experienced at BDSM than you; they'll be happy to teach you good form and technique, but they have no reason to tolerate a top who pushes limits or doesn't have control of toys or equipment.

AFTERGLOW

It may seem daunting at first, but the protocol involved in visiting an SM professional is all designed to satisfy your needs while keeping you physically and emotionally safe. You may need to visit several professionals before you make that perfect connection – or you may find that the first woman you meet is the mistress or submissive of your dreams. Do some research, develop a language to describe what you want, be communicative, and respect your own needs and limits – as well as those of the domme, sub or switch you're visiting. Be prepared to encounter a variety of personalities, and be willing to conform to the rules and procedures of any dungeon you visit. With these skills, a little courage, and an open mind, I trust you'll find that the professional dungeon can be a wonderful resource, where lifelong fantasies can be realized.

Phone Freaks

by Lord Master Damien

Other contributors to this collection will undoubtedly focus on their interactions with clients in the flesh. I prefer to concentrate on what I have found to be the most curious aspect of being a professional leather Master – the all-important initial telephone interactions with potential clients.

Like any form of sales, a dominant's work is a numbers game. Maybe one out of ten calls actually results in a paid session in my dungeon. But those are just the facts of a salesman's life. Many callers are merely requesting information and are not yet ready, if ever, to book a session.

No, what contributes to my dimmer view of human behavior is the bane of every sex worker's existence: non-serious callers, derisively referred to in the profession as phone freaks. These time-wasters come in several distinct species. If you're serious about wanting to book time, with me or any other pro dominant, then please don't follow their examples.

There are the guys who make appointments for two hours later, then don't confirm at the set time for the directions. This happens maybe two out of every three times someone books an appointment. Why make the appointment in the first place if you have no intention of keeping it? I'm sure some of these callers can't afford my fee and are too embarrassed to say so, or they're newbies and simply chicken out. But those explanations hardly cover all such callers. And how hard is it to call back and cancel?

There are several, almost sure-fire markers that tend to give the time-wasters away. There are the guys who say, "Money is no object"; the guys who say they want to watch me fuck their wives; and anyone who identifies himself on the phone as slave bill, or slave bob, or slave anybody for that matter. Anyone who says any of these things is a sure-fire bullshit artist. And when one caller combines two or more of those lines – as happened to me just this week – it's all I can do not to laugh.

Then there are the ones who have unblocked phone numbers and repeatedly call to make appointments they don't keep. Uh, hello? Don't they realize I recognize their numbers? Apparently not.

Another common species of non-serious callers are the dreaded "phone wankers." As the name indicates, these jokers call me up while staring at the photos in my ad, and try to keep me on the line long enough for them to get their rocks off. But they easily give themselves away with their heavy breathing and excessive, repetitive questions about my dungeon, my equipment, or our impending session. Bye-bye now. Gotta go.

Then there are the truly bizarre phone encounters that defy categorization, such as the following classic conversation I once had.

"Hello?" I answer.

"Master Damien?" the caller asks.

"Yes."

"Hmmm..." and then he hangs up.

Huh? Can someone please explain that one to me?

Then I had a lunatic caller named "Larry" who, after a couple of no-shows on his part, I would merely hang up on. He would call back and plead for me to give him another chance, arguing that his flaky behavior had been caused by some unspecified drugs he had been on.

"I'll give you $1,000," he would promise, which is much more than my normal tribute.

I would decline his offer, of course, telling him that given his track record, his only option was to send the donation to my P.O. box ahead of time. Once I received it, then I'd be willing to make another appointment. He would dutifully take down my P.O. address and promise to send me the money... which of course, he never did. But did that stop him? Of course not. He would call back a few days later, asking if I had received the money, knowing full well he had never sent it. I would say no, he would swear that it was in the mail, at which point I would curtly tell him to call back in a few more days. "Why are you being like this?" he would implore, all hurt. "I'm being real with you."

As of this writing, "Larry" has apparently gotten the message and has stopped calling me. But knowing him, I'm sure he'll be checking in with me again any day now. Can't wait.

The worst phone freaks, however, are the ones who make an appointment, call back at the scheduled confirmation time (usually two hours before the session) for the directions, dutifully take the directions down... and then never show up. Statistically, this happens maybe one out of every seven times that someone calls back to confirm. What is that about? Even more egregious are the ones who call back to confirm, show up as instructed at the gas station right around the corner from my dungeon five minutes before the scheduled session, call for the exact address (I never give out the precise address until they show up at that gas station), then never take that last step to my front door. This happened just the other night. Some guys change their minds at the last minute, and that I can understand. But the others obviously have little if any life.

Whatever. As they often say in Mafia-themed movies, "This is the life we've chosen."

So here's how callers to professional dominants should behave on the phone.

First and foremost, be very polite and very respectful. Think of the call as a job interview, one in which you're trying to make a very favorable impression. This is a top you're calling, and you should treat him or her as such.

Call at a reasonable hour. Not early in the morning and not late at night. We tops keep normal hours, and we most definitely do not sit by the phone 24/7 waiting for your calls at 2 a.m. If our ad specifies a time to call, call during that time – no sooner, no later.

Book your session as far in advance as possible. We tops are not short order cooks.

When the top answers the phone, say something along the lines of, "Hello, Master. This is (fill in your name). I saw your ad in (the specific publication or website) and I'm inquiring about a session." Do not call the master or mistress "honey" or "baby" or "sweetheart" or the like. Do not cop any kind of smart-aleck or sarcastic attitude.

Do not bombard the top with a lot of time-consuming questions. A few questions are okay – such as the general location of the dungeon and the top's availability – but you should be able to tell from the top's ad and/or website most of what you need to know before you call.

Certain questions are absolutely verboten. Do not ask for the top's age or his or her measurements. (It's somewhat less offensive to ask a male top his cock size, but do not, under any circumstances, ask a mistress her breast size.) And absolutely do not try to negotiate down the required tribute. Seeing a professional top is an expensive pastime, and not everyone can afford it. If that's you, save up your money and only try to schedule an appointment once you have enough.

Do not interrupt a top when they are talking. If a top asks you a question, answer it. Do not answer a question with a question, such as:

Top: "When would you like to session?"

Caller: "Where are you located?"

Obviously, do not play with yourself when talking on the phone with the top (we'll know most of the time). And do not whine about the traveling distance to his or her dungeon. If you really want to see this particular top, any reasonable traveling distance is well worth it. If it's not worth it, don't complain – just say "No thanks" and end the call.

If you get the top's voice mail, you may leave a message, but do not expect the top to call you back. The onus is on you to call the top back.

In short, when dealing with a top, the ball is always in our court. We come first, you a very distant second. It's all about us, not you. If that doesn't turn you on, then serving a master or mistress is not for you.

Guidelines for Successful Online Negotiations

by Cléo Dubois

You have made up your mind. You are ready to visit a professional dominant. Perhaps it is your first time ever; or perhaps you think you have done your homework by browsing a BDSM site that lists mistresses in your area. Perhaps another mistress has referred you to a trusted domina. You put your fingers on the keyboard and start the email that will be your first contact with her. What do you say? Where do you start?

My first rule of successful online negotiations is to really do your homework. You've visited my website. Did you really read what I say about myself and what I offer, or did you just glance at the pictures? Most of the mistresses I know take great care to make sure our sites clearly represent what we are about. If you don't read them, thoroughly, and take them seriously once you have read them, you will be wasting your own time as well as your potential mistress's. On my site, there are listings of the seminars and workshops I teach, as well as the various sessions I offer for individuals and couples. You can purchase and even preview my videos, and find links to other informative kinky sites. All of this is there to give you as much help as I can in choosing your personal path of erotic S/M exploration – and to free up some of my time so I can teach those workshops and do those sessions! So why send me an email requesting a video, when my website clearly tells you how to order it directly?

If a mistress's website lists her interests and your fetish is not on her list, she is most likely not into it. For example, I do not do baby scenes. So asking me to be Mommy and put you in diapers is wasting my time and yours. So is asking me to secure a slave girl for you in Nebraska, when I am in San Francisco and do not mention anywhere that I provide this service.

Let's say you enjoyed my pictures, read about my work with individuals and couples, and signed up for my newsletter. Now you want to contact me for a session. I have a question for you: How many emails do you get a day? How many do you think I get? If I read all my emails every day, I wouldn't get much work done, let alone have any fun. Everyone is overloaded with spam these days, and sometimes it looks so real! A friend of mine recently sent out an invitation that I never received: not because it didn't get to my mailbox, but because I didn't recognize her address and it came with a title that sounded like spam. So if you want me to notice your email, be direct and relevant in the subject line. "Session inquiry" or "session request" is a lot better than "your slave is waiting" or "down on my knees." "Guided Play Session Wanted," "Sadist, Need Training," "submissive training inquiry": these are concise and informative headings that will definitely attract my attention.

Once you have created an informative subject line for your email, you really need to make yourself clear. As concisely as possible, tell me your first name, a bit about your past experiences in BDSM (or lack thereof), what you're looking for, and when you'd prefer to have your session. It may be tempting to be creative, vague, or evasive, but the more informative you can be from the start, the sooner we'll be able to connect.

Someone who writes any of the following will receive my reply:

Dear Ms. Dubois,

Thank you for allowing me this letter of introduction. I'm a 38 year old submissive male, with experience since 1995. I do not often travel to SF or other large cities. When I do, I try to seek out the most experienced, well-equipped, intelligent professional. I will be in SF Oct 26 & 27 and would like to discuss the possibility of an extended session on one of those days. I have read "Different Loving" and feel I know something about your style, interests, etc. I visited your website and love all the pictures you posted and how you speak about your work. My main interests include bondage (shackle and chain preferred), cbt (especially gadgetry) and nipple play, electroplay, and moderate corporal, maybe a little bit more than moderate with the right mistress. I look forward to your reply and hopefully we can speak at your convenience.

Yours,

f—

Dear Ms. Dubois,

I am pretty much a plain vanilla guy. I have been attending munches (for a few months) and have been to one class at Janus. I have a "significant other" who lives out of state and who I'm lucky enough to see several times during the year. She has an interest in erotic spanking, and I would like to learn to please her in this way. Therefore, I would like to find out if you could train me (a bottom, I'm sure) to deliver an erotic spanking for my dear lover? If this is something you would endorse, then I need to know if I can afford your fee.

Thank you for taking the time to read this. I hope to hear from you soon. Oh yes, I will be seeing my S.O. next in early to mid June, and I'd like to be trained by then.

Best regards,

b—

Dear Madame Dubois,

My friend B— suggested I talk to you. My partner, who I love dearly, wants me to beat her up and I am afraid to hurt her. It's not that I'm weak or can't do it, I'm just afraid that if I let go of my power, I will hurt her. That seems to be just what she wants.

I noticed on your Website that you offer guided play sessions in the privacy of your dungeon. I am interested in how long those sessions are and what you charge. As you can tell, we are new to BDSM. We have read "Different Loving" and we will be in San Francisco next month for a two week holiday. Is there any chance you would be willing to help us?

Best regards,

L—

These emails are clear, respectful, and brief. In a few words, I know who, what, why, where, when and how. Our negotiations have begun.

On the other hand, how do you think you represent yourself when you send your scripted fantasy to a total stranger, saying it is for Her and Her pleasure? Who do you think you are fooling? Here is what I mean:

Dear and sublime Mistress,

I am on my knees begging to serve you. I need to worship your lovely patent leather 5 inch high heels while you cane my bottom and then bend me over your spanking horse, tying only one of my

hands so I can masturbate for Your Pleasure while you spank my naked bottom with your gloved hands.
      Your devoted slave,
         J—

Furthermore, nothing is more of a turn-off than receiving a four-screen-long email that starts with, "O Mistress, I am your devoted slave. Here are my likes and dislikes," followed by a detailed laundry list, like you are ordering an *a la carte* fantasy feast! Also, don't just copy and paste those long negotiation forms found on the Net. Have enough class to send a personal email.

As you can see, when it comes to online negotiations, my best advice is to be direct, be real, and be yourself. It will show.

Here are a few more general tips:

Remember to give me a return email address that only you will see. Don't send your mail from an address that I can't reply to without endangering your safety and confidentiality.

If the mistress you wish to visit doesn't have the information you need posted on her ad or website, please ask if she is interested in your fantasy or fetish.

Keep it short! Describing every session or fantasy you ever had in great detail is not the way to contact a mistress.

It is okay to ask a professional dominant about the length of her average session, her fee, and what she really enjoys in the dungeon. In fact, it is more than okay: it is appropriate.

If you have been seeing another professional mistress, it is okay to mention it to the new domina you are contacting.

If you have no intention of visiting a mistress for real in her dungeon/playroom, do not be a time waster. Please. Yes, I said please. There is much online domination available, so use those services instead. If playing online with webcam mistresses is your cup of tea, that is fine – but do not waste the time of women who are offering dominance in person.

Above all, respect your kinky needs, and respect those who understand them and dare to provide them safely for you.

So as you can see, truly, negotiating online is not much different than negotiating face to face. Just one last thought: the Internet has created a whole new language, and new opportunities for communication. Along with those opportunities come many pitfalls, and the ability to lie is one of them. It's easy to create an imaginary portrait of your abilities. But I have to warn you: We play with a dangerous edge in BDSM, erotically, physically, emotionally and even spiritually. This is no place for lies.

The next step will be a phone conversation. Be centered and calm, and *do* ask, do tell and do listen. When you are naked before the woman you choose to dominate you, I wish you a deep and erotic exploration of your kinky needs.

Beatings R Me

by Mr. Sleep

My specialty is choking and savage beatings. So, as a man of the sensitivity required to deliver the best misery money can buy, I have certain pre-stated strictures that will make my time making your time miserable, just a little bit nicer. For me, of course, you ass.

1) Lose the Jennifer Lopez CDs before I come the fuck over. Nobody wants to hear them, much less see them, and it just serves as a constant reminder to me that I should have gotten an MBA, instead of squandering my time on MBAs with ass-lashing fetishes, such as yourself.

2) No sandals. I hate them and you should too.

3) Don't act like you forgot this is a cash transaction. We're not friends. You don't do it on the bus, so don't do it here.

4) No sudden moves. It might get someone hurt. And I'm not talking about feelings.

5) Same goes with "surprises." We don't like them in real life and certainly not while doing outcalls.

6) You asking me if you can suck my cock fifteen times in a row is one way to meet Mr. BallGag, because:

7) *No sex* in our ads means *no sex*. Not a Clintonesque variant of *no sex*, but no cocky, no sucky.

8) *No*, I do not want anything to drink. I don't trust you that much.

9) Telling me how beautiful I am won't get me to let you suck my cock.

And last but not least, we'll end this on a positive note:

10) Fight back all you want. It won't help.

How to Treat a Sub: Take Pride in Ownership

by Joy James

How do you treat a submissive slut slave? Sounds like a rhetorical question. You should be able to treat her any way you want! Verbally humiliate her, physically degrade her, use her as a cumhole, and then inflict pain when she doesn't behave – right?

Well, yes and no. For nothing is as simple as it first seems in the sex trade, and power transfers get even more complicated.

For starters, it's both easy and extremely hard to find a true – total and complete – sub. Easy, because there are a lot of subs out there, just waiting and yearning for their proper master. They'll even pay to be dominated. Now comes the hard part; it also has to do with money. Let me try to explain:

I once ran an ad – for fun, not for money – in the "Personals" section of the local alternative newspaper. It read something like this: "Slut slave looking for macho dom to fill me up and tell me what to do." I was inundated with responses. So when I turned pro, I ran the identical ad in the "Adult Services" section. Unlike the "Personals," which are free, this new ad cost me $150. But I got one – count 'em, exactly one! – response. Go figure.

And then I ran a paid ad offering my services as a dominatrix, specializing in forced feminization. (Like most girls in the business, I can switch roles.) Guess what! I got an incredible return on my investment. Again, go figure.

I've spent a lot of time trying to figure it all out myself, and I've spoken to a lot of other working girls about the subject. All have had dom clients for whom they've played the sub role. But none specializes as a sub, even when that role might in fact be their personal predilection. It's just too limiting, and fraught with complications. That was the general consensus, the reasoning behind which I'll now share:

On some level, any sex worker is by definition a submissive. Even when the sex worker is playing dominatrix, the client who pays for the service is ultimately the one in charge. As in any retail business, the customer is always right! The service worker's mission is to serve/service him, right?

But paradoxically, when you pay for the services of a sub, right away you shatter the fantasy that she's your slave. If she really were your property, no money would ever change hands. The converse – to pay a dominatrix – just reinforces the fantasy. To pay someone to humiliate and degrade you adds to the submissive pleasure; you're such an unworthy slave, you even have to give the mistress money. Maybe that helps explain why, from a sex worker's perspective, the market for subs-only seems so soft, and why it doesn't pay to limit one's repertoire strictly to the submissive side.

Then there's the fear factor. I'll never forget one guy who wanted to act out a mock-rape scenario. His script was elaborate, every detail of which he forced me to memorize – from the clothes I would wear (including the style and color of my panties) to those items of clothing he would rip off me and thereby destroy (whose cost I calculated as part of the fee). He even provided a lengthy description of the cord he would use to tie me up so he could then sodomize and rape me.

But what he never warned me about were two stinging slaps of his hand across my cheeks. This unscripted violence, happening right after he had tied me up, instantly and involuntarily brought me to my knees, as well as tears to my eyes. The expression of shock and fear on my face that he elicited was no doubt exactly what he desired. But his thrill would be fleeting, for I now refuse to go out with him ever again – despite his many phone calls and entreaties, plus his stated willingness to double my normal fee.

So my unsolicited, humble suggestion to clients is simple: Treat your sub like a movie star. You're the movie's director, of course, my master. But don't go changing the script. Don't be tempted to improvise. That doesn't mean you can't explore limits and boundaries with your leading lady. But you must also give her every chance to say "no."

Just because I've agreed to painful nipple clamps doesn't mean my master should bite my breasts. Just because I'm compliant when it comes to spanking doesn't mean my master should force a huge butt plug up me as well. Just because I'm poured into a latex bondage hood and catsuit so tight I can hardly breathe doesn't mean my master should smother me with a pillow. Maybe you can bite, maybe you can plug me, maybe you can even smother me, but let's at least talk about it first. And listen when I say "no." "No," whether in a single word or a code we've agreed to beforehand, means "no."

If you're too disappointed, you can even have your money back. To paraphrase the immortal words of another leading lady, Greta Garbo, just leave me alone.

It's not about the money. Well, not only about the money. It's about power. And as such, your exact relationship with a sub requires a delicate dance of constant negotiation. Having the persuasive skills of a diplomat can help.

A sub is your property. Take pride in ownership. Look after us and ensure that we're not permanently hurt or broken. Like any owned object, we shouldn't have to have a mind of our own. You must think for us, and look out for our best interests. A true master should never have damaged goods.

P.S. Bring your own paraphernalia. The sub might well have her own mask, inflatable cock gag, and cuffs, or whatever, but don't get mad if she doesn't!

Paying For It

Phone Sex and the Internet

Phone Sex Basics

by Delicious Dawn

Many phone sex customers are unaware that good phone sex is a two-way street. Phone sex is only as good as you make it; it's an interaction between the customer and the operator, not a solo performance. Many customers call with unrealistic expectations and no knowledge of how to proceed, and they don't get the best sexual experience that they could.

It's not uncommon for us to get a call from someone who says "Hello" in a quiet meek voice and then just sits there in complete silence, expecting the phone sex operator to satisfy him, without giving any clue as to what he wants or whether he's turned on. But we're not mind readers. Every man has his own unique desires, fantasies, fetishes, etc., and what works for one customer may not work for the next. So it's important to let your operator know what you're looking for and what's arousing for you. It's best to do this at the very beginning, so she knows where to start. Do you want oral, anal, a threesome fantasy, a good hard fuck, a nice slow fuck, lovemaking, domination, a naughty neighbor fantasy? Or a combination of several of these?

If you enjoy something varied like domination, then you should give some specific details about what kind of domination you like. Some domination fans may want to be controlled and ordered to worship the phone sex operator's pussy and ass. Others want to be fucked in the ass, and still another may want clamps put on his nipples and clothespins on his cock and balls. So if you want a good ass fucking and don't enjoy pain, or you love worshipping pussy and wouldn't dream of getting fucked in the ass, and you don't tell this to your phone sex operator, then you may not get a satisfying experience.

As the call proceeds, you need to keep letting her know if what she's doing is working. Let her know what turns you on. If you don't feel like using words, then make moans and groans, or "oh yeah"s of pleasure, to signal her. If she does something that's not a turn-on for you, then guide her where you need her to be instead of hanging up on her.

If she asks you a question, answer her. Sometimes I ask my customers something like, "Do you like to have your ass licked, Baby?" and they just sit there and say nothing. Or I ask, "What are you in the mood for, Baby?" and they say, "I don't know," or, "Anything and everything." These kinds of answers make it very hard to know what to do next.

Phone sex customers need to know what turns them on, and they need to express that. The operator and customer should respond back and forth, just as if it were a real sexual encounter. Interaction keeps the momentum going, and feedback from the customer is essential to keep the sexual energy flowing. It's just like physical sex. If you were licking a woman's pussy or fucking her, and she didn't say anything or even make any noise, you wouldn't know if she was enjoying it, and you'd lose interest. The same applies for the phone sex operator. No one wants to have sex with someone who doesn't say a word. If you want enthusiasm, you need to give enthusiasm. Come on guys, don't be a dead fuck! If you contribute nothing to the conversation, you aren't going to get a quality experience.

A common misconception in this business is that any customer should be able to click with any operator, and she'll always be exactly what he wants. This is not realistic. We can't and don't connect well with every customer. Just as in all human interactions, we click with some people and not with others. This is not a reflection of our skill as a phone sex operator – it's simply human nature. So if you find a phone sex operator who doesn't do the trick for you, then politely tell her that it isn't working and that you'd like to try someone else. Don't just hang up on her.

It's also very frustrating when men hang up abruptly after they come, or right before they're about to come. Sometimes with very quiet men, we may not even know you've come and hung up, and we keep talking until we hear that familiar buzz in the phone that tells us you're no longer there. Then there are the ones who hang up abruptly in the middle of the conversation when they're about to come, giving us a loud and annoying click in our ear. I have several regulars who obviously enjoy my service since they call me repeatedly; and yet every time they call, they hang up on me as soon as they finish. For goodness sakes, guys, at least say "thank you" for the service you've received. Hanging up without saying "goodbye" or "thanks" is incredibly rude. It really takes only a couple of seconds to complete the call with a polite thank you, and you'll be greeted more enthusiastically the next time you call.

You should also be aware that you're calling a real woman, in her home, which means she's going about her life between calls. We have graciously opened our lives up to you because it's a turn-on for you to speak with a real woman at home. So be respectful of her time. Don't waste my time with one-minute calls, interruptions from children or wives or co-workers, or bad cell phone connections. Make sure you're not going to be interrupted and that you have enough money in your account. I sometimes have callers put me on hold right in the middle of the call to answer the door, put more money in their account, answer their call waiting, or attend to children crying in the background. This is distracting and not the right condition for a steamy phone sex encounter. Find a place to be alone, where you won't be interrupted, and have adequate time to devote your full attention to the call. You wouldn't like it if

I put you on hold to answer my call waiting, or if my children were crying in the background.

And please don't interrupt me at 2 am for a one-minute call. I love to wake up and have a hot exciting call with an enthusiastic customer, but I don't want to be interrupted for someone who's already breathing heavily and jerking his cock, doesn't bother to give his name or say anything, and hangs up on me in one minute.

Along this same line are the men who sneak into a bathroom or another room of the house to get away from their wife or lover, whispering so low that the phone sex operator can't hear them. I sometimes get guys who are so quiet I can't hear a word they're saying – and who then get pissed and hang up. Other guys speak in a low whisper because they're shy, uncomfortable, or ashamed to be calling a phone sex line. You must speak up, guys, and call under the right conditions!

Another thing that really cuts the quality of your call is cell phones. If at all possible, don't use them. They often don't have a good connection, and it's hard to be a hot little sex kitten when your customer is constantly breaking up and you're speaking to the airwaves half the time. It's also incredibly frustrating to lose your customer when you're really on a roll, just because the cell phone lost its connection. If you must use a cell phone, make sure you have a quality phone and that you're in an area where interference is at a minimum.

The customers I enjoy the most are also my most satisfied customers, and they share the following qualities:

They like to chat with the phone sex operator briefly and make some kind of human connection before getting into the sex. It's nothing too personal and extensive, but there's a little getting to know one another. There needs to be some kind of connection for a call to be the best.

They know what they want and what turns them on, and they know how to communicate this to the operator.

They interact with the phone sex operator as if it were a real physical sexual encounter, responding with words or sounds that let the operator know if she's on the right track.

They have a good sense of humor. Some of the best calls are when we laugh together. This is often a great way to begin the call, as it breaks the ice and creates a connection.

They are enthusiastic and active participants.

They always say thank you before hanging up. For some customers this may be a simple and quick "thank you" right after coming, and for others it may include some intimate talking and cuddling. But at the very least, there's an expression of appreciation for what they received.

How you treat your phone sex operator will affect the way she treats you and what kind of service you get, and will go a long way to helping you have a hot, sexy, and enticing phone sex experience. If you follow these basics, your operator will appreciate it, and she'll respond to you in a more exciting and positive manner. When we like a customer's behavior, we give much more, and we go out of our way to make his experience exciting and fulfilling.

So, guys, before you pick up that phone and make that call, get to know yourself sexually. Be sure of what you want and what arouses you, learn how to express it, and educate yourself on proper phone sex manners. If you want a hot phone sex tryst, you need to invest something in it other than money. You're paying for a service, so make the most of it!

Letter to a
Phone Sex Client

by Jessica Melusine

H ello, honey.
You've seen the advertisement, had some hot thoughts, and now you're ready to call, to enjoy some hot talk or explore a new fantasy.

I'm on the other end of the line, and I have a few tips for you.

As a phone sex operator, I talk to clients ranging from the delightful to the difficult. With some clients, I looked forward to their calls every night, and what I learned from them can help you be the kind of client a phone sex operator dreams of. So listen. I know you want to.

Know what you enjoy and ask for it. Most clients – and operators – want their telephone time to be filled with actual hot talk. If we have to spend a lot of time figuring out what makes the client hot, it can be very frustrating, both for us and for you. Phone sex operators are not phone psychics, so do some thinking about what turns you on before you call. It'll help make the call a hot, sexy experience rather than a frustrating one. If you want to talk about oral sex, or you've always had a fantasy about being dominated, tell us right away. And if you aren't sure, take a few moments to chat about what you might want, instead of waiting for us to guess. You'll spend much less time negotiating, and much more time having fun.

Make sure your operator can hear you. I have received phone sex calls from army bases, factories, garages and office cubicles. It's hard to give a client what they're asking for if there's outside noise, whispering, or a bad connection. If you're calling from a loud or unusual location, make sure your operator can hear you. You'll have a much more satisfying experience if we can understand your sexy words.

Be courteous. Phone sex operators look forward to polite and courteous clients. Being nice will definitely get you extra attention! If your operator needs to take your billing information, be patient; this is probably dull for him or her as well. And if you've had a lovely time, please say so; it feels very gratifying when I get a "Thank you" or even a "That was so hot." Expressing your thanks and being patient will make you someone your operator loves to talk with.

Have your billing information ready, and be patient while it's verified. If you're calling any kind of phone sex service, there will be a billing period where either an automated system or an operator takes your billing information. Please have your driver's license (or other ID) and your credit card or checkbook handy, so you can give the appropriate info without slowing things up. And if your billing information or phone number need to be verified, be patient; we're doing this to ensure that your credit card or checkbook hasn't been stolen. Please don't leap to the sexy talk before the billing is done – you'll get no response, and you may even have your call terminated. Being patient and courteous during the billing process gets you a much lovelier time when you finally get to chat with your own operator.

Give feedback. The only way an operator can tell what you enjoy and don't enjoy is through your voice. So let him or her know. If there's something you want to hear about, or particular words or sounds you like, tell them. Personally, I love getting feedback, so I know that my client is having a great time or is discovering something they enjoy. I've also learned a few new things this way!

Enjoy yourself. If you've decided to explore phone sex, take the time to enjoy yourself. Imagination and auditory stimulation can be a deeply arousing and fun experience. So, while remembering all these other ideas, don't forget that this is pleasurable – and if you approach it that way, you'll have a great erotic experience. Place your call, relax, and have fun.

Thanks for listening. I'll be waiting by the phone, and I do hope we'll be talking soon.

Seductively yours,

Jessica Melusine

World Wide Websex: Doing it Right Online

by Taliesin the Bard

Porn is everywhere on the Internet these days, in many forms, from live interactive sex shows to sexy chat rooms to racy newsgroups. To be a truly successful cybersex surfer, you need to know what works and what doesn't with the providers of pornographic pleasure, the people on the other side of the Webcam. I've had a little experience in this area, so let me share with you some of what I know.

Did you note that I said "people" in the above paragraph? That's right. Those are people to whom you are jerking off. And what they're doing is their job. Acting sluttishly, masturbating and moaning for your enjoyment, is what they do to pay the rent, put food on the table, provide for their families. Some might enjoy the work. But remember, always: for the live sex performers, Webcam women, and technicians who make it possible for erotic entertainment to be transmitted to you in the privacy of your own home, this is work.

They're professionals. If you show a little respect for their profession, you'll go a long way. For example: Saying (via chat) "I really like the way you finger your pussy, it's really turning me on" to a young lady with a Webcam pointed at her splayed open legs is a compliment to her professionalism. Saying "You dumb cunt, shove more fingers inside yourself" is not.

Live interactive shows allow you to make requests. So feel free to do so. Ask – I repeat, ask – her to put more fingers inside herself, if that's what you want. If she can, she will. She wants to make you happy, wants to make you cum. And she wants you to stay around long enough so she makes some money. She'll give you a good show if you let her.

Please, though, don't get disgruntled if she can't deliver on every request. She may be your fantasy for the evening, but she's only human. Recognize that, and treat her as a person; a naked, willing-to-please person, but still a person.

Here's a little Websex history to put this in perspective. In the late 1990s, companies in Canada and Europe had begun transmitting commercial hard-core sex shows via the Internet. In the United States, however, we lagged behind for some time, with only softcore and simulated sex. There were hard-core pictures, and some prerecorded video content, but apart from swingers and other uninhibited spirits sending signals for free, there was nothing live. The commercial transmission of hard-core sex was a risky proposition in 1997.

Always one to advance the art form (and to have the opportunity for hot sex with some of the most beautiful and horny porn women around), I partnered with some Internet tech people to do the first US commercial live transmission of hard-core sex over the Internet. Cherie LaVeaux and I performed that show: the first time anyone had paid to see a live sex show originating in the United States via the Internet. We soon had a solid following of fans, and some of the finest performers in XXX displayed their erotic talents for these live shows – Carole Troy, Bunny Bleu, Fiero, Purple Passion, Eden, Jeff Dickman, Liza Harper, Montana Gunn, Rod Fontana, Candy Vegas, Heather Lynn, Dallas, Valentino, Sophia Ferrari, Red, Chris Cannon, Randi Storm, Alyssa Allure and others. (Fortunately, some of those shows were preserved on video, in six volumes titled "Live Sex Now" by Odyssey Group Video.)

I performed occasionally, but with the operation in full swing, I eventually had to attend to directing the shows and managing the studio. This position put me in contact with the fans watching from the privacy of their own homes. Never had there been more immediate feedback to an XXX performance than the messages sent by chat and e-mail from the viewers. The World Wide Web provided immediate interaction. Via chat, viewers could suggest sexual positions they wanted to see, or camera angles they preferred. (The "point-of-view" angle, in which the actor held the camera with the actress performing fellatio or other sex acts on him, was particularly popular. The image on screen appeared to be from the point of view of the viewer, and anyone watching could put himself in place of the actor and easily fantasize that it was his dick being sucked, not mine or Rod's or Red's.)

The computers we used allowed us to transmit video and audio signals. However, we could only know what the viewers were saying by what they typed into the chat software to us. The fans always had requests, and we tried to accommodate them as best we could.

One thing that really surprised me was when the viewers began requesting to see the chat operator, to see what she (or he) looked like. Hard-core sucking and fucking was going on right in front of them – twosomes, threesomes, and foursomes, women with women, oral sex, anal sex, occasionally an all-out orgy – and they wanted the camera turned around to see who they were talking with, even if it was one of our male crew members. It makes sense when you think about it. Everything that happened was filtered through the chat operators: they were the ones the viewers were most directly connected with, and of course they wanted to see them.

Our main chat operator was Isis. She wasn't a regular porn performer, and she normally dressed in casual clothing, but she would occasionally wear lingerie while chatting. Sometimes, if politely requested, she would spread her legs and show her pussy or bare her breasts for the Webcam. Even when she was dressed casually, the fans wanted to see her. And she had many fans. As the contact point with our audience, she was quite popular, and an essential part of attracting new viewers to our shows. How the viewers treated her was quite important – she was the one who relayed the requests to the performers.

One thing she did was to treat returning fans to private chats using the software's "whisper" mode. In normal chat, everyone participating in the chat sees all messages, whereas "whisper" mode was used for private communications. Fans who were regulars and who were polite, not pushy or overly demanding, got the favored "whisper" treatment from Isis. Remember, even over the Internet the rules of common courtesy apply. So be polite and friendly. It gets you further than anything else. (Isis, amazingly, was able to handle close to a dozen private conversations while at the same time maintaining the regular chat.)

Nobody performing sex wants anyone to tell them to change positions every ten seconds. "Suck his dick. Put it in her ass. Now do it doggy style." You'll get to see all those things if you're patient. Give the performers a chance to get a rhythm going, to build up some heat. You'll get a better show that way. Sex performers are professionals, but they're not machines or robots. You can't flip through sexual positions with live performers like you can flip channels on the TV or fast-forward with a VCR.

Of course, we did occasionally run into a few problems, including computer crashes, requests for sexual acts that we just couldn't provide at the time, and fans who didn't believe that what they were seeing was live. Live sex shows were such a new idea in the late '90s that many people had trouble believing what they were seeing. When we could, we'd have one of the actresses who was performing say the names of various people who were watching, or we'd write a person's name on a sheet of paper and hold it up in front of the Webcam. Some people still had trouble believing. If a person was rude about it, or told us we were lying when we said we were live, he got no favors from us.

Because we had a number of viewers at the same time, it was sometimes difficult to get to all the requests, and some people tuned us out, not believing that we would fulfill their requests. We tried to keep everyone happy, but the viewers who got frustrated and didn't stay with us lost out. We had some of the best performers working in XXX at the time, and the viewers who stayed with us got to see that. Those who were patient got to see some of the hottest sex ever, and in essence got to play amateur directors, instructing the performers in what to do. Imagine being a porn fan and being allowed to direct a hard-core XXX scene featuring your favorite porn star. What a thrill!

It was a lot of fun doing the live shows. We made many porn fans happy, and broke new ground. I like representing the community of XXX, with its proud lineage dating back to the days of the sacred prostitutes, and its modern traditions of defending freedom of speech and expression. Sharing one's sexuality, making others aware of the permutations and possibilities of their own sexuality, and helping people to explore their erotic natures, is a joy I wouldn't have missed for anything.

The Suicide Girls Are Alive and Kicking Ass

by *Serena Lucine Verseau*

You can see me clothed in tattoos and accessorized with piercings and missile-pop hair on SuicideGirls.com, a softcore site for goth, punk and emo mamas with a notable lack of inhibitions. Log in, scroll down, and click on Thora (as in thorazine), and you'll see my profile. I filled the blanks in myself. No one edited it, nasty-ized it or reinvented my kinks, and it's not just about sex; in fact, it barely touches on it. I laid my favorite movies, books, and interests out for all pervs to see. My career, my cat, and my crush on Kali are cozied up to a foxy headshot and a list of friends I talk to on the site. You can leave me testimonials, comment on my journal, even email my private box – everyone's doing it. But you've gotta play nice if you want to last.

When writing me email, don't, for the love of Goddess, ask me to marry you; it's just bad manners. It's the Internet, we've never even seen each other's mice. And while we're there, don't suggest I have your baby, cure your virginity, or perform your next astral blowjob. Worship if you must, but keep to your side of the temple.

Suicide Girls like polite compliments, devoid of neediness. While we're arguably remote healers, we are not therapists. You might think we're the best thing since Real Dolls, but there are some voids we don't want to fill.

Specific is good, but we don't want your input if you haven't got past how our muffs are groomed. Acknowledge all our dimensions, at least the ones we've let you in on. For instance, instead of typing, "Damn! You're hottt! Are those your real boobs? Sheeeeit, I'd like to take you home to Mama. I'm not coming on to you or nothin', I swear. I just like masterbatin' (sic) to your pics," try, "Hi, I visited your photoset today, and, wow, you're stunning! I thought I'd take a minute to say 'hey' and express my utter gratitude to your mother. ;) Seriously, the energy that comes through in your pictures is wicked sexy, and you have terrific style – I love the pink patent cuffs. It seems like you have a lot of cool interests, too, astrophysics, poetry... I checked out your profile and noticed you read The Tao of Pooh, and I don't know anyone else on the site who listens to Sopor Aeternus. Well, I just wanted to touch bases, and if you feel like writing back, I'd be over the moon."

See, now, isn't that better? A little netiquette goes a long way, and there's nothing hotter than a mature and spellchecked e-voice. Consensual back-and-forth mailing is pleasant and fulfilling: just remember your boundaries and don't ask for personal information, like place of residence, STI status, or legal name. If I'm going by an obsolescent brand of anti-psychotic medication, chances are I don't want members to know I'm named after Aunt Prudence in Modesto. Informing me that you'll be out my way for a visit next week will more likely appear creepy than cordial, and dropping into headquarters for a SG reunion will only get you a date with a man in uniform and a big stick.

Never ask a question twice. If it doesn't get answered the first time, that's a clue. You don't need to know if pierced nipples run in my family or if I'm really a lesbian. I can only accept that I'm the most beautiful woman you've ever seen if you've actually seen a woman irl. Don't offer me modeling contracts, recording deals or replacement skulls for my parasol unless you are going to follow through. Fakes and flakes suck badly, and it quickly becomes clear when someone is trying to create a dependency.

Not all criticism, no matter how well meaning, is constructive to us. If we want your photoset suggestions, we'll ask, and if we need your advice, we'll write. I had a guy e-drool over me, asking me when my next set was going up and whether I'd be barefoot in it. Now, I like a good fetish, but finding a letter like this in my personal inbox felt plumb icky. While SuicideGirls thrives on its sexually charged content, writing sexually explicit letters to a model is improper. Getting to know a SG one-on-one demands healthy distance and common courtesy. On SG we are poppin' fresh dough, three-dimensional – no, make that four, with the dimension of mind. We are holographic, not hollow, sentient, not solely sexual, and as heard as we are seen.

There's a newly subbed member who goes down the SG list and posts coarse comments in our journals, such as "You should dump your loser boyfriend and let the Marquis whip your topping." He asks moronic questions, like "How did you get so bald down there?" and challenges male members on the quality of their "game" and how much of it they've got. Word on such cads will spread, so if you're inclined to mess with the Girls en masse, don't expect us to keep your secret.

In a similar vein, there was a guy who copied and pasted "Post something in my journal" to every last Girl. In his entry, he boasted that he was conducting an experiment to see how many SG's he could get to write him. Needless to say, the dude is on a lot of our "to avoid" lists. Less idiotic, but still annoying, was a member who mass-posted "What is ugly?" While the question itself had philosophical merit, the entropic act of copy-and-paste was a turnoff, and although I had quite a bit to say to him, I didn't reply.

Bragging is as distasteful as begging. I once got a message from a member with whom I'd never interacted, and it was obvious he was trying to impress me. I clicked on his profile and saw that he'd listed his IQ in his "stats." All it did was incite me to list "People who don't put their IQ in their stats" in the "Into" section of my profile. Even the lauding of horsepower and penis prowess is better stomached than that of standardized test scores.

SG is a community, and the discussion boards and special interest groups are further proof of this. They're loaded with flirtatious banter and heavy debate, dirty jokes and snarky stabs, high praise and small suicides when a thread burns itself to a dead star. SG is easy, colorful, accessible, and fun, but there's soy between the buns. We're fabulous, feminist, and scary smart, and we enjoy a good fight. But all is not fair in board warfare. There's no asylum for bigotry, and the fool who goes there will face prompt zotting. Racism, sexism, and homophobia are never okay, nor are body-type bashing and ad hominem attacks. If you tend toward any of the above, don't let the log-out feature zap your ass on your way out the door.

Be polite when arguing your point. It's intellectually healthy to disagree, but remain respectful to the person with whom you're debating. Don't attack a SG or member's honor because you don't like hir views on the ethics of Nike buying out Converse, or paper vs. plastic. There will be days when you'll have to step back from a thread, and sometimes it's better to be graceful than right. But there are those posters who rub us like a cheese grater. There's this one guy who defends pedophiles in every related thread. I don't think he's condoning the act of pedophilia, but he does seem to go out of his way to uphold the rights of child molesters and extol their humanity.

Ass kissing is as visible as a boil on a butt and transparent as the empress's birthday suit. When a member predictably posts ingratiating comments in response to anything written by his favorite SG, it's nauseating. In a similar vein, when embarking on a losing-your-virginity thread, don't contribute unless you've actually lost it. I can't tell you how many times I've stumbled on a thread about first times, incredible orgasms, or whatnot, and some desperate whiner comes in with "I'm still a virgin" or "My ideal sex partner is any woman who will have me."

Don't use the site to promote your band if you're a no-good sneak. There's this kid who starts threads with compelling subject lines, which, when clicked on, reveal a link to his band. He plays it off like it's some random group he's keyed up about and solicits input from the Girls and members. This is about as wrong as guys who post pictures of themselves naked in penis-size threads. They're the ones who end up looking like dicks.

I will say this: the support systems that weave themselves as thoughtlessly as silk bring tears to the voyeur's eye. It's absolutely mind-boggling that a porn site could give you a shag, a hug, and a smile, all in one sitting. It's nothing short of revolutionary.

You are children of the universe and we are all connected, so if you don't want to lose your connection, read the FAQ and learn your boundaries. You'll be glad you did when my new set goes up and there's an extra pussy shot or three. (I posed with my Siamese cat.)

So kick off your Converse and stay a while. I got a new tat and pierced some more parts, and with our numbers increasing every day you'll be swimming in a sea of Suicide sirens. And now that you know how to worship me like the Goddess I am, come on over and drop me a line. Who knows, I might even write you back.

Fringes

What to Do When
You Meet Me

by Nina Hartley

I meet a lot of people. You could even say that I'm a professional people-meeter. The people-meeting aspect of my job was, for many years, more time-consuming and profitable than my main gig, the reason that everyone wanted to meet me in the first place: being a porn star. I did the math once and came up with the conservative estimate that, at the height of my touring and convention-going, I came face to face with about thirty thousand people a year, most of them men. I can honestly say I've met all sorts of people, in all sorts of places, doing all sorts of things. I meet them at the supermarket, at the airport, at the bank, at clubs, at conventions, gallery openings, press conferences, and university classrooms. With these kinds of numbers, I'm bound to meet people with good manners and those without them. If you are a consumer of adult material, and you make efforts to meet your favorite performers at clubs, conventions, and the like, I have a few tips for you.

Different venues dictate the need for different approaches. But some things always apply:

Don't be drunk. You're *not* as charming as you think, and the courage the booze gave you to tell me something important will be wasted on the fact that I can't understand what you're saying – as well as the fact that I'm already annoyed and hoping you'll just go away.

Don't expect sex. Sure, joke and flirt all you want. That's in our job description, and we like to do it. But we're professional fucks, and we don't usually pick someone up at work. It has happened, of course, but when it does, it has little or nothing to do with you. If we want you, you'll be the first to know. Unlike civilians, we really can't be sweet talked into bed, and our bullshit detectors are usually turned on "high."

Don't expect the character you see on screen. Remember, we're performers. In real life, we're smaller and more normal than you think we'll be. Our feet may hurt, we may be tired, we may be handling a personal crisis... there may be any number of things going on that distract us from the sexual nature of what we do. We shine on screen, on stage, and on the microphone. But off duty, we're just women and men.

Don't try to peddle a script idea. That's not our department. Besides, the industry doesn't want your script *at all*. The companies that use writers already have all they'll ever need or use.

Don't try to peddle yourself as a performer. We'll just direct you to A.I.M., the industry health clinic (see the Resource Guide in the back of the book), so you can call and get the bad news from them: it's next to impossible for guys to find their way into porn, and it's actually impossible for the average dude with average equipment who doesn't already know someone in the business.

Ditto for passing yourself off as an up-and-coming producer. The road to bankruptcy is paved with the carcasses of guys who only wanted to make a "good porn film because there's so much shit out there." Besides losing their money and their sanity, they don't even get laid.

And ditto for wanting to improve the music in movies. The reason the music sucks is that the producers don't care and just rely on music from the public domain. The very few producers who do score music already have the musicians they like best.

There are two main categories of places where you may meet up with someone you recognize from porn: official porn-promotion events, and just out in public. How you should approach us depends on which kind of place you see us in.

If we're in public, just use common manners. In a supermarket, restaurant, movie theater, gym, etc., wait for an appropriate moment and be polite. If you're absolutely sure of who it is, you can extend your hand for a shake and say, "I love your work!" If she seems amenable, you may even ask for an autograph. Have your own paper and pen, as we don't usually have them on us. Don't ask us for a date, which will make us blow you off. If you're not quite sure (it's easy to be confused when she's wearing a cap, sweats, and no makeup), approach politely and ask, "Excuse me, are you on TV?" or "Are you _____?" or something to that effect. Give us room to be anonymous, and don't push it. If you see us with our kids, or people who seem like they could be our parents, think twice about approaching, as we may snub you.

On the other hand, if you meet us at a strip club where we're featuring, you have a great opportunity to have close contact with the star of your dreams. If you sit at the stage, *tip!* You may be rewarded with boobs in the face. Clap enthusiastically, but don't overwhelm her show, or she'll hate you. When it comes time for her to do Polaroids, get in line and pay the fee. She'll sit in your lap and you'll take a nice photo. If it's slow, or you're last in line, you may get many minutes of her social time, if she's in the mood and likes your vibe. If you have a bunch of stuff for her to autograph, definitely wait to be last, so she won't rush you and you won't make the guys behind you angry and restive. Added insurance would be to bring your female partner, as we always like couples and usually give them extra time. Don't be upset if we flirt more with your wife than with you – we're trying to get you laid later!

It's somewhat different when you meet us at an adult convention. There are adult expos and video conventions held throughout the year in different places. For these events, a company will hire us to be in their booth to sign autographs and pose for photos with fans. Bring your own camera, as there won't be Polaroids. We'll be dressed provocatively and we'll be happy to see you; we'll hug you, take a picture with you, sign any magazines you've brought, and some of us will even look at your kid's baby picture. Depending on the star, the placement of the booth, etc., she may have a huge line (in which case you'll be lucky to have ninety seconds with her), or none at all, which means you'll get to talk with her for as long as she'll let you. At the conventions, we're being paid to be friendly, upbeat and happy. This is the main place where we meet the folks who actually watch our videos, and we want to know how you like us.

That about sums it up. Meeting your favorite star can be a wonderful moment, and it can even lead to true friendship, but don't expect it to happen that way. Meeting her can also be the biggest bummer in the world, as is true for any person you know only from the screen. Keep your expectations realistic, and you'll have more fun when you do run into your favorite porn star.

Dildos by Phone

by Greta Christina

S o let's cut to the chase. When you're shopping for mail-order sex products, why should it matter how you treat the people who answer the phone? I mean, they aren't like regular sex workers, like prostitutes or pro doms, who can and do turn down customers they don't want to work with. No matter how obnoxious you are to the person at the sex-stuff-by-mail company, it isn't going to affect what shows up when the UPS driver arrives with your package. It's not like we're going to refuse to sell to you... right?

Well, in extreme cases, we might. I worked for a mail-order sex product catalog for many years, and there were, in fact, some customers who were so outrageously vile that we put a red flag in their customer records, noting that we should never, ever sell anything to them ever again. The one who responded to being told he couldn't return videos by calling us "cheap Jews," for instance. And the one who hysterically raged that we'd been deliberately deceitful and even fraudulent for claiming that a video's performers were attractive, when by all objective standards they clearly were not. (More on him later.)

But those were extreme cases, and there were damn few of them. In the years I worked for this company, we put "Do

147

Not Sell To This Schmuck Ever" flags on the files of maybe half a dozen customers. So again I ask: Why should you care? How exactly will being pleasant to the nice lady or gentleman who's selling sex products over the phone get you better service?

Here's the thing. If you know exactly what you want to order when you pick up the phone; if you're positive you know what you want as a substitute if something's out of stock; if you don't have a single question about anything you're order- ing; and if you have no special requests whatsoever about shipping or handling... then yes, the way you treat your order taker probably won't affect anything but your karma. But if you need *anything* in the way of special service – if you have questions, if you need advice on what to buy or how to use it, if you want an exception to a company policy, or if you need to be 100% sure that your package arrives by Bastille Day – then being a pleasant customer is going to make a world of difference.

So here are some guidelines on how to be pleasant to the nice people who sell you dildos by mail.

The first thing to remember is that the people at the sex products company are not offering free phone sex. As far as I know, nobody in the world (except maybe your sweetie) is of- fering free phone sex. Now, if you have actual questions about actual products in our catalog, by all means call us up. At the company I worked for, we prided ourselves on our ability to answer questions, offer advice, and generally help shepherd customers through the ordering process. The people on the phones knew the products well – much of the time, we'd tried them personally – and if we weren't familiar with something, we'd find someone in the office who was. But we also prided ourselves on our ability to identify wankers. Folks who work for sex product companies are sharply attuned to the differ- ence between people with legitimate questions, and people who just want to talk to the 800-number person about sex. So if you're trying to get your rocks off listening to a girl (or a guy) talk about dildos, we'll cut you off the minute we've figured you out. And if you keep trying, we'll keep cutting you off. If dirty talk is what you're looking for, do us all a favor and call a phone sex line. The folks there will be happy to talk about dildos with you all day long.

The sex product company is also not a free sex information hotline. This may be a more painful point to accept, but it's true and it's important. Again, at the place I worked, we were always happy to answer questions about the stuff we sold: either before you bought it to help you decide what to get, or after you got it to help you figure out how to use it. So if the dildo you bought keeps slipping out of the harness, or you want to know which lube is best for anal sex, then by all means, give the sex toy company a call. But if you just have questions about sex in general ("I want to try butt sex but I'm afraid it'll hurt," "How can I talk my partner into trying bondage?"), please don't call the sex shop. Yes, they sympathize with your desire for information: but it's not what they're there for, they have other work to do, and you're probably calling on their 800 number, thus making them spend their own money to answer your questions. So don't bug them for general sex advice (unless the advice you want is contained in the books and videos they sell). Call San Francisco Sex Information instead. They are, in fact, a free sex information hotline, and they do exist solely to answer your questions about sex. (Their contact info is in the Resource Guide at the end of this book.)

There's a basic principle here. The sex toy company is trying to run a business: so calling about business is generally fine, and calling about non-business annoys them. But there was a very common, completely business-related question that annoyed the heck out of us – namely, male customers asking advice on what to buy their wives or girlfriends. These guys would always want to speak with a woman, and they'd always ask us to explain "what women like." Now, I appreciated that they wanted to make their sweeties happy in bed, and I always helped them as much as I could. But what they didn't understand is that not all women are the same. I mean, just because

I'm a woman doesn't mean I know how to get your girlfriend off. The reason we carried over a dozen vibrators is that different ones work better for different women. While I know these guys meant well, I always felt a little insulted by them. Maybe I'm being unfair, but it seemed like they thought of all women as sexually interchangeable. If you want to know what kind of sex toy or smut video your honey would like, I strongly advise you to ask her. (Or him.)

So those are some things to avoid. What about the up side? What positive things can you do to make your dildo phone person happy? Well, for starters, patience is definitely a virtue. If your phone person needs to put you on hold, or if the vibrator you want is backordered and your order's going to be delayed, try to be understanding. If you have time concerns, by all means let them know – but don't be an asshole about it. Trust me, they're not any happier about the delay than you are, and they're not jerking you around on purpose for their entertainment. They want to make you happy and sell you things if they can. That's how they stay in business.

Compliments are also nice. If there's something special you like about the company, or if you really enjoyed the last video you bought, let the person you're talking to know. And if your particular phone rep has given you special service or just been pleasant to deal with, tell them. It'll make their day.

But there is such a thing as being too friendly. Getting a lot of personal questions can make a phone rep pretty uncomfortable, especially in the sex product business. Personally, I was usually willing to answer questions about my own sex toy or smut video experience, as long as the questions were clearly meant to help with an order. But not everyone at the company felt that way. And if the customer was asking which buttplugs I liked just to make sexy chit-chat, even I got the willies. So if you really need personal testimony about the Anal Intruder, try to make your questions as businesslike as possible – and be willing to take "I don't feel comfortable answering that" for an answer.

And there's definitely such a thing as being *waaaaaay* too friendly. I had a few customers who always asked to talk with me and me alone, and they always wanted to chat at length, telling me the details about the last toy they bought and how much they admired my taste in porn. They were probably harmless, but they still creeped me out a little. You never know when a fan is going to turn into a stalker. With a couple of these guys, it got to the point where I didn't want to talk to them at all, and I'd consistently punt their calls to another staffer if I could. Pretty much a textbook definition of "self-defeating behavior." So if you have a crush on someone at the sex toy company, do try to chill it out.

Anyway. Back to the positive side. Like I said, being patient and understanding makes a big difference. It's important when something isn't going right on our end: if the vibrating cockring you want is on backorder, or your package hasn't arrived when we said it would. But it also applies when we're doing everything right and are following all our policies to the letter – and you're just not happy about it.

Here's an example of what I mean. At the company I worked for, we had a firm policy that videos or DVDs could never be returned unless they were defective, and even then they could only be replaced with a good copy of the same title. We had a good reason for this: there's a common scam in which people buy videos, make copies to keep or sell, and then return them for a refund. So even though we'd let people return other stuff that they just didn't like (even if it was something like a dildo that we'd just throw out the minute it got shipped back), we were firm about videos and DVDs – No Returns. (Most mail-order video companies have the same policy.)

But we got a call one day from a customer begging us to make an exception. She and her husband had been happily watching a video we'd sold them, when an actor came on the screen who looked exactly – exactly, she emphasized – like her father-in-law. It wasn't actually him, but the resemblance was too close to be anything but creepy. She and her husband were immediately wigged out and completely turned off, and they were sure as hell never going to watch that video again. She explained the situation – and we happily let her return the tape.

Why did we make an exception? Well, partly because we were sympathetic, and partly because we were entertained – we'd definitely never heard this one before. But the main reason was that she was so understanding about it. She got the humor in the situation, and she started out by saying, "I know you have a 'no returns' policy on videos, and if you can't make an exception I understand, but..." If you want a business to make an exception to a policy, those are the magic words. A company doesn't typically make rules and policies just to piss off customers – the rules are there for a reason, usually to keep us from being ripped off and to let us stay in business. If you understand that we're not just being randomly tight-assed meanies, if you can make a good case for why we should bend the rules in your situation, and if you're nice about it no matter what our answer is, there's a much better chance that we'll let the rules slide for you.

Oh, and speaking of videos that turn you off. We would, in fact, accept a return on a video if our description of it was inaccurate (if, say, we'd described an incredible blowjob scene with Annette Haven and John Leslie, and it turned out that this scene had been cut from the version we were carrying). But a comment like "You said the video was hot, and I thought it was boring" does not count as a complaint about inaccuracy. Different people like different things, and while we always made a great effort to describe our videos fairly and in ways that made it easier to shop (raunchy or artsy, rough or gentle, plot-driven or wall-to-wall sex), the bottom line is that we can't promise that any given video will get you off. All we can promise is that it got us off.

On that topic: Probably the most common complaint we heard about videos, and easily the most annoying, was "You said the performers were attractive, and they weren't." As if there were a perfectly attractive porn star in a vacuum in the

Smithsonian, against whom all other porn stars could be objectively measured. I had a customer berate me once on this topic, at great length and in very nasty personal language. We'd described the performers in a video as attractive, and when he got the tape, he discovered that it hadn't been cast with gym-toned, long-haired, large-breasted twenty-somethings. Now, we'd clearly said in our description that this wasn't a mainstream video and that the performers weren't professional porn actors. Anyway, see above, re: personal taste not being objectively measurable. But this guy was convinced that there were universal standards, accepted by everyone in the porn industry and the porn audience, about which qualities did and did not make a porn performer "attractive." (I swear to God, I'm not kidding – he was serious as a heart attack.) He simply would not believe that we'd found this video's performers eminently fuckable. He felt we were being deliberately deceptive and even fraudulent, and he said so, at length, and in increasingly abusive language. So he got the red flag. No more dirty videos or sex toys for him. Not from us. Not ever.

My point isn't just "don't call the dildos-by-phone person a lying bitch" (although that is a valid piece of advice). My point is that if you're trying to get an exception to a "no returns" policy, don't do it by insulting our taste. It will get you less than nowhere – it will piss us off, it will convince us that you're an idiot, and it will make us less likely to help you, not more.

There are some more mundane details that make a difference as well. Know what you want before you order; have a second choice ready in case your first one's backordered; have your credit card in your hand when you call. But these apply to any mail-order business, regardless of whether you're buying vibrating buttplugs or polo shirts. So I won't bore you with that stuff. It's mostly just common sense, anyway.

Finally, be aware of the type of place you're calling and what their vibe is. I worked for a fairly small, personal company, and a lot of the ideas I've been discussing are based on that. If you're ordering from a big, glitzy outfit, don't expect the same kind of personal attention, flexibility, or willingness to answer extensive product questions. And of course, the converse of that is also true – if you want to buy your sex products from someone who cares about their work and can give thoughtful answers to your questions, stick with the smaller, more personable companies. There's a list of them in the resource guide in the back of this book. Have fun, and happy shopping!

Out of Your Head and Onto the Page

by Sage Vivant

The very best thing about writing customized erotica is the physical distance I maintain from each and every client. I admire sex workers who give clients access to their bodies – or their psyches – because I know I wouldn't have their fortitude.

I supply clients with one, six, twelve, or twenty pages of erotica, based on their own unique and specific sexual fantasies. They answer a few basic questions so I can get a sense of who they are and what they like, then I craft what I hope is a memorable tale. I've operated Custom Erotica Source since 1998, and during that time, I've been happy to indulge fantasies – safely and from a comfortable distance.

And yet, there's no question that I experience a certain emotional coziness with anyone who orders a story from me. People divulge fantasies they've had for years, and I provide them with a story that takes that fantasy one step further, or crystallizes it in a way that their imaginations alone won't allow. I get to know their sexual peccadilloes as intimately as their partners do, and in some cases better. I crawl inside their heads long enough to learn where the erotic switches are, then

I crawl outside again to duplicate that unique control panel in a story.

Maybe most sex workers would find my job as scary as I find theirs.

The vast majority of my clients are courteous and polite. I enjoy almost all of them and admire their courage in revealing their sexual fantasies to another human being. Many of my clients have made me laugh, made me think differently about certain sexual endeavors, or helped me learn more about myself. Most of them are ordering stories for a significant other to celebrate their relationship, and the rest want delicious little indulgences they can enjoy by themselves.

But how they establish their first contact, with either me or Custom Erotica Source, determines what kinds of difficulties I might encounter with them. Since I began the business in 1998, I can count on certain behaviors.

INTERNET CONTACT

Ninety-five percent of my contact with clients occurs over the Internet. They find CES online, they peruse the website, they place the order, all via cyberspace. If they haven't spent enough time on the site to understand what "custom" means, if they haven't read the range of sample stories that represent the wide range of fetishes and interests that CES can serve, and if they don't have the time to consider their needs as thoroughly as they should, these are the types of requests I might get:

"We like everything! Surprise us!" Nobody likes everything, nor do I have time to incorporate everything into one short story. When I read this type of request, I then have to write to the client and ask some carefully targeted questions to find the one or two sexual hot buttons that should be showcased in their customized tale. My advice: Try to narrow your story requests down to a couple of particularly compelling ideas, so I don't guess wrong about which of fifty different fetishes you might enjoy most.

On the other end of the spectrum, the customer might provide a twelve-page request designed to help me write a six-page story. This means I must extract the truly relevant details from the twelve pages, and then write a condensed version of what the client has already written. I marvel at the inefficiency of this process, and wonder why anyone would want an abbreviated version of what they've just created themselves. Too much detail is worse for me than not enough, because it means that the fantasy is cast in cement – and for a writer, trying to capture what's already vivid in the client's mind is fraught with anxiety. How can I get everything right? You've had decades to finely hone this fantasy, but I have only a few weeks and partial information. If your fantasy is so involved that describing it takes more paper than my eventual writing, you might want to consider whether you aren't more qualified than I am to do your tale justice.

And finally, there are story requests that are little more than sex scenes devoid of any plot or apparent point. Writing about sex is what I do, but what I hope distinguishes CES from the ubiquitous smut-story websites is the extra dose of sophistication that transforms a sex scene into a sexy story. Story orders that describe sexual positions as their primary focus disappoint me and my writers, because there's no opportunity for eroticism. I've often wished that I could tell people that when sex has no context, it can't be anything but dull, puerile, and downright pointless. But because I have to give them what they believe they want, my hands are often tied. I keep hoping some of the sample stories on the site will inspire them to think beyond mere positions, but it seems that some folks are rooted in some fairly pedantic notions about what erotica is all about.

BY PHONE

Some clients don't like to type the nuts and bolts of their fantasies into the website's questionnaire, so they prefer to phone me. When they call, they also take the opportunity to ask me questions about the process, the timing, the look of the final product – all valid inquiries, to be sure. One would assume that a person who favors the phone over the Internet would have an affinity – or at least a talent – for articulating their needs. Sadly, this is frequently not the case. I once spent nearly fifteen minutes asking question after question to determine what a client wanted. The conversation progressed as follows:

"I want to give my husband a story for his birthday. Something about us."

"Great! What would you like to see happen in the story?"

"Oh, you know. Something romantic."

This is the point where I grab a handful of hair and squint, as I strategize the line of questioning that will elicit some specifics from this willing but shy client.

"What does your husband like to do? Does he have any hobbies?"

"Yes. He surfs."

"Do you surf with him?"

"No, I don't like the beach."

"What do you like to do together?"

"Go out to dinner, the movies – stuff like that."

I try to keep my sigh inaudible.

"Has he ever confided a sexual fantasy to you? Have the two of you talked about something that you'd some day like to try?"

"No," she says cautiously, "not really."

I try to remind myself that this caller must have had something in mind when she dialed my number. I am increasingly determined to find out what it was.

"Is there anything in particular that turns your husband on?"

"Just the usual stuff."

"Maybe a certain position? Dirty talk? Dressing in a certain way?"

"Well, yes... maybe you could have him dress in a French maid's outfit."

A-ha! Paydirt. Yet I can't help but wonder why I had to pry the information out of her. I write off most of these conversations to client discomfort, and I certainly understand that the experience is most certainly unlike any they've had before. Nevertheless, having some idea of what you want before you place an order would save everybody time and energy.

IN PERSON

This kind of contact is exceptionally rare for me – and that's by design. When people hear what I do for a living, eyebrows are raised. When the eyebrows belong to a woman, I also get a sparkle in the eye and that conspiratorial lowering of the voice that implies, "Oh, that must be fun!" They want to hear about what it's like to give life to other people's fantasies, how I got into this line of work, and if it affects my personal life.

Men, on the other hand, immediately assume that I am a prostitute, dominatrix, sex surrogate, or any number of other professions that would require me either to get naked for them or force them to get naked for me. Once and for all, guys, my body is off limits to you, and I have no interest in pursuing yours.

I once attended a meeting of a local association of entrepreneurs. The meeting was pleasant; people blushed, people gushed, people asked questions. One woman, a dentist, said she thought an erotic story starring her husband and herself might be just the thing to rekindle some passionate embers. I handed out business cards – and collected a few – and felt it was a night well spent as I walked to my car.

"Hey! Wait!" A deep voice bellowed behind me. I turned around to observe one of the attendees, a tall, dark financial consultant, sprinting to catch up with me. Though he was nearly out of breath by the time he reached me, he didn't hesitate to speak.

"So." Pant-pant. "That's some interesting business you've got there."

I may have been in businessperson mode that night, but the woman in me was also very much present, and she couldn't miss the way he leered at me.

He leaned in close and introduced himself again. Lawrence was his name. I shook his hand quickly. "You're brave to come tonight. If my wife knew somebody like you was here, she'd never let me come back to one of these meetings!" He chuckled. By himself.

I knew he did not understand my business. I knew I should explain that I do not provide a sexual service of the physical kind. But I wanted to get away from him more than I wanted to clarify my business plan.

He showed me that he had my business card. "I'm going to save this," he promised. "Some night when I'm in the city, I'll give you a call and we'll have some fun. Would that be okay?"

"Sure, sure," I said hastily, squeezing into the driver's seat of my car as quickly as possible. I could have added, "and I'll just hang up on you," but time was of the essence.

Lawrence kept his promise, and did indeed call my business line several days later at one o'clock in the morning to find out if we could "get together" at some hotel I'd never even heard of. I deleted the message, grateful he didn't have my home phone.

I am a writer who writes about sex and sexual situations. I'll write your fantasies and make them dance in your mind's eye for as long as you care to keep the story on your shelf, but I will not dance for you. My power, as well as my comfort level, lies in the physical distance my work affords me. Through the words you put on a page, I learn not so much about who you are as who you think you are. Through the words I put on a page in return, you become that person, and then some. But to get the kind of story that will endure, the kind of story you'll pick up every few weeks to feel good about yourself or gain some insight into your sexual nature, you need to take a little inventory before you contact me. Have some idea of what turns you or your loved one on, and be able to express it so I can grasp it and mold it into a story you'll love. Recognize that if it's a prostitute or sex therapist you want, trying to turn a writer into one could take a very long time – particularly if that writer insists on being a writer exclusively.

So rest assured that I don't insist on this physical distance between us because I dislike you. On the contrary. Keeping your body away from mine allows me to read your erotic mind, which is the stuff of truly memorable stories.

That Couple

by Stephanie Anderson

About eight years ago, I was the BDSM/magazine/porn anime purchaser for an "adult" store in Minnesota. I was also a clerk. Most of my shifts were spent dealing with people who didn't understand how to use a cock ring; listening to peepshow booth clients bitch about how they got ripped off; telling people "Only one person per booth" (which I thought was stupid); busting shoplifters; busting people trying to fuck in the bathrooms; tracking down comics, magazines, 'zines, and obscure materials about sex and BDSM; figuring out how to hang sex swings; and other fun activities.

While clerking one insanely busy Friday night, I had a couple approach my counter and ask for some advice. She was slight, dark-haired, pretty, and walking with a cane. He was your average blandly good-looking man. As a couple, they seemed like your average suburban married folk, looking for a way to spice up their lackluster marriage. Par for the course.

I had to deal with some rude jerks before I could answer their questions. On this particular Friday, I was working in the gay/lesbian/bi/trans area of the store. I had frat boy assholes roaming around with their cheerleader girlfriends, looking at gay video boxes and making rude and obnoxious comments. I had to shout at them, "Look, you moron, it says 'Triangle Books and Video,' get it? That means GAY. If you don't like it, there's the elevator, you small-minded little pricks. Get the fuck out of my store!" Namecalling ensued and security had to be called. This was the norm for Friday nights. The local university was close to the store, and after the bars closed, all the drunken idjits came into the store for a cheap thrill. They never bought anything except whippits and poppers.

When I finally got the store cleared of the morons, I went back to the couple who were browsing the vibrators. The woman approached me, and I smiled and apologized for the delay. She was a little flustered but not hesitant at all. She said, "I want to look at the biggest vibrators and dildos you have available."

I was a little stunned. I smiled and showed her a few that were, in my opinion, huge. After looking at them, she said, "Is that it?" I asked if she had something particular in mind. She looked at me and her eyes started to well up with tears. The man was standing by her the whole time; he put his arms around her and said, "She has MS, and one of the first things to go is sexual sensation. I am her lover and I want her to get off a few more times before she is totally unable. We are looking for something that would help us with that."

I picked up the biggest dildo and the most powerful vibrator. I said to use them at the same time, that using them in combination should help her achieve some sensation. I told them that if it didn't work, they could come back and go through my catalogs with me to find something that would be more useful. And I said that even though we had a "no return" policy, I'd let them return it if they were unsuccessful.

They didn't come back.

It was a hard, low-paying, and shitty job. Customers like that couple, who made me feel like I really helped them with something sacred and important, were rare in the adult industry. It is definitely at the top of my list for favorite sex-industry moments.

Paying For It

Afterword

A Live One

fiction
by Greta Christina

What an asshole, Sheila thinks as she plays with her pussy. He's been popping quarters into the booth like they were rock candy. A smile wouldn't cost anything extra.

She smiles down at the customer through the glass, a sugary, seductive smile full of bubble and promise. He responds with the same blank stare he's been giving her for the last five minutes. His face is flat and listless, a cheap cement statue of a gloomy frog, with a faint trickle of hostility leaking through the stone set of his mouth.

She sighs and spins around, giving up, turning her face away. She sticks her butt in the window and runs her hand slowly over her ass. The fucking brick-wall men, she thinks. I've never understood why they come here. I mean, I can give them the sight of a dancing naked woman, but I can't give them the joy of watching a naked woman dance. Don't they get that they have to bring that themselves?

She licks her forefinger and runs it up and down her pussy as she gyrates her hips to the thumping music. She catches Tanisha's eye and gives her the contemptuous look she can't give the customer. Tanisha gives a quick nod of sympathy and turns back to Danielle. The younger girl is sprawled over Tanisha's lap; she squirms and rolls her hips dramatically, putting on an extravagant show for the two drunken sailors in the corner booth. Tanisha scowls ferociously and slaps Danielle's tight, round rump; Danielle gives a theatrical squeal and wriggles in delight.

I like a girl who enjoys her work, Sheila smiles to herself. She knows these two; they'll be doing the real thing later on. They love faking the guys out, but they never do it for real for money.

She hears the panel slide down behind her, and glances over her shoulder. Yup, he's gone. What a tragic loss to the human race. She arches her back, sore from bending over, and looks around dutifully for a new customer.

Sure enough, just as she finishes stretching, the panel in the other corner booth slides up. She glances at Lorelei, who's busily spreading her pussy for a middle-aged man with a briefcase in one hand and his dick in the other. Guess the new one's mine, Sheila concludes. Conscientious as always, she shimmies over, squats in front of the guy, and smiles. "Hi," she hollers over the deafening synth-pop din. "I'm Chloe."

In response, he pulls a pad and pen out of his pocket and begins scribbling. He holds it up to the window and smiles back. *Hi Chloe,* it reads. *I'm Henry.*

Her eyebrows shoot up, surprised and impressed. Smart guy, she thinks. Inventive. And he actually wants to talk to me. Maybe this will be a live one.

She tucks her legs under her like a cheesecake model and runs her hand over her torso. "So, Henry, you come here often?"

He writes furiously and holds the pad up again. *Yes,* it says. *That's why I brought this. I know it's too loud in there for you to hear me...*

He flips to another page and scribbles some more. *But I want to be able to talk. This is the best I could come up with.*

He reaches into his pocket and drops a handful of quarters into the slot. She ducks her head and blushes; she knows she should know better, but she's always a little surprised when guys drop their money just to look at her. She licks her finger and runs it over her nipple. "So, you like me?"

Yes, he writes. *You seem... friendly.*

She leans back, spreads her pussy lips open for a teasing moment, then lets them close again. "I try," she answers. "So what would you like to talk about?"

You.

"Sure," she smiles. "What would you like to know?"

He thinks for a moment, then scribbles again. *What part of your body do you like best?*

Her eyebrows shoot up again. "Interesting question. No one's asked me that before."

Really? Nobody?

"Well, nobody in here," she shrugs. "But to answer your question, I'd say... my ass. I like my ass a lot. Would you like to see it?"

He scribbles hastily. *Sure I'd like to see your ass...*

He flips to a new page. *But I want to see your face, too.*

"You got it, bub," she says cheerfully. She leaps to her feet, spins around, flops over at the waist and gapes at him between her legs. "How's this?" she grins.

He laughs and shakes his head. *That's really silly,* he writes.

"You're right," she answers. "I never understood that one either. Okay... let's try this."

She gets on her hands and knees, putting her body in profile. She gives him a smoky look over her shoulder, tousles her hair and growls. Tiger woman, she thinks. Queen of the jungle. She shifts her leg to show him her soft, round ass, arches her back, and grinds her hips in slow circles. "How's that?" she asks.

Much better, he writes. *So what do you like doing with your ass, Chloe?*

She doesn't hesitate. "I like to get it fucked," she replies crudely.

Show me.

She puts her finger in her mouth and draws it out slowly, getting it nice and wet. An unexpected shudder goes through her body as she raises her eyes to meet his. His gaze trails down her back like gentle fingers, and she squirms and wriggles, pleased and flattered and oddly bashful. She reaches back with one hand, opens her asscheeks invitingly, and runs her wet finger up and down the crack. He gazes back at her face, solemn and anxious; she gives him a small, coy smile and waits.

Please?

She grins and licks her lips. She wets her finger again, then slowly slides it into her asshole.

A sudden rush of pleasure rolls into her head. She moans and closes her eyes, almost against her will, as she slowly pumps her finger into her ass. A small, tight spot in her throat begins to dissolve, melts down into her breasts and stomach; she bucks her hips up hard, bites her lip, and begins to whimper quietly. Her ass clenches tight around her finger, pulling it in deeper.

She opens her eyes suddenly, remembering where she is, and gives Henry a wild, intent look. His hands are pressed against the glass, clutching the notebook; his eyes are open wide, shining with lechery and delight. She shoves a second finger into her asshole and begins to fuck herself in earnest, hard and crude and a little rough, just the way she likes it. She moans louder, throws her head back, and lets out a sharp little cry of bliss.

She collapses onto the floor, panting dramatically. She rolls onto her back, pulls out her fingers and surreptitiously wipes them onto the grimy carpet. "Oh, my god," she whispers.

He takes a deep breath and pulls away from the glass. *Jesus, you're beautiful*, he writes. *Thank you.*

She props herself up on her elbow. "You're welcome."

Was it real? he writes.

"Mmmmmm," she murmurs. "You bet."

Really?

She hesitates. "Well... yeah," she says uncomfortably. "More or less. I mean, it felt good. Felt real good, actually. But no, I didn't come, if that's what you're asking."

He smiles and nods. *Thanks for being honest. I appreciate that.*

A softer song comes on the jukebox. *So, do you like working here?* Henry writes.

The lie springs to Sheila's lips, the automatic lie hammered into her by months of unspoken training. She gives him a long, serious look, looks around to make sure nobody is listening, and speaks.

"Well... here's the deal," she murmurs, as softly as she can and still have him hear her, as loudly as she can without being overheard.

"Yeah, I do like it. The money's good, and the hours are flexible. I don't have to work forty hours to pay the rent. And the dancing itself is fun. I like to dance and I like my body... and I like sex, I like being sexy." He grins and waggles his eyebrows. "And the other women are amazing. They're smart and funny, and they really take care of each other. I just love them to pieces."

But... he writes.

It all comes out in a rush. "The fucking men," she says bitterly. "They want it all spoon-fed to them. Pussy and pleasure and all the rest of it. They think sex should be like TV, but with hotter babes and no commercials. They just wanna sit back and suck it down like baby birds. They don't smile, they don't say hi, they don't say 'Thank you' or 'You're pretty' or even 'Nice tits, baby.' They just stare like dead fish. Not all of them... but a fuck of a lot of them." She takes a deep breath, startled by her own anger.

He nods. *Men are assholes,* he scribbles.

She laughs heartily, her bitterness broken for the moment. "Thank you," she says. "So... what would you like to see now? Anything special?"

What would you like?

She chuckles. "Why don't you take your clothes off and dance for me," she jokes. "Just for a change."

He scribbles seriously for a long minute. *Okay. But I'd better warn you, I'm not a very good dancer.*

He sets the pad on the bench, runs his hand through his hair, and slowly begins to undress. She stretches out like a cat and watches in awe, amazed that he took her seriously.

He unbuttons his shirt, slowly, caressing his chest as he uncovers it bit by bit. She plays with her own body in response, moving her hand over her belly as he strips off his shirt and shows her his thin chest. Hesitantly, he begins to roll his torso in slow, snakelike ripples. She can smell herself, the sharp, salty smell her pussy gives off when it wants something really badly. She watches hungrily as he slides his hands down over his hips. He begins to rub his dick through his jeans, and she draws a sudden, ragged breath. Her pulse beats hard inside her clit; she shoves her hand between her thighs and squeezes tight.

Suddenly he stops dancing and snatches up the pad and pen. *I feel silly,* he writes. *I feel like a dork.*

She shakes her head, baffled. "You shouldn't," she replies. "You look great. I'm getting totally wet watching you." She stares meaningfully at his crotch. "Now show me more."

He drops the pad and pen, slumps against the wall, and gives her a moody, smoldering stare like a model for designer jeans. She laughs and nods approvingly. He begins to move again, squirming against the wall. Slowly, teasingly, he unbuckles his belt, unzips his fly, and tugs his swollen dick out of his pants and into the open air. He cradles it in his hand and gives her a wide-open look, proud and fearful and eager for approval.

She ogles his cock and licks her lips, drinking in his eagerness like water. "Very pretty," she says. "Very nice indeed. But I wanna see more. Turn around and pull them all the way down. Show me your ass."

He complies immediately; he turns to face the wall, and slowly pulls his jeans down over his slim hips. She whistles appreciatively as the fabric drops to his thighs and his bare ass is revealed. He blushes bright red, presses his hands against the wall, and bends over to give her a better look. She stares intently at his ass, relishing his exposure, sucking in the view like a starving woman. Her clit thumps hard, demanding attention, and she begins to caress it in earnest. *I love a boy who does what I tell him,* she thinks.

"Now turn around again," she commands. "Let me see your dick. Let me see you jerk off."

He spins around to face her, jeans around his knees, face flushed, his dick twitching of its own accord. He jams his back against the wall, licks his hand like a dog, and begins to slide it up and down the shaft of his cock.

A sudden flash of longing stabs into her cunt, and she whimpers and spreads her legs wider. She opens her pussy lips with her fingers and thrusts her hips towards the glass, frantically and insistently, forcing her hole into the open, trying to show him as much of herself as she can. His eyes widen as they take in her sopping wet cunt; he grips his cock with a trembling hand as she spreads herself apart and furiously rubs her swollen clit. Their eyes connect; they stare intently, flushed, shivering, mouths hanging open, eyes wide. His hand moves faster and faster; a shudder travels through his body, and he bites his lip, throws his head back, and squirts into his hand. She sees his face contort, and cries out hard, and comes.

They both take a deep breath and slump backwards. Sheila stretches back and clamps her thighs around her hand; Henry collapses against the wall, lost in quiet bliss. At last he pulls his pants up, takes a handkerchief out of his pocket, and wipes the come off his hand. He picks up the pad and pen. *Thank you thank you thank you,* he writes.

"Jesus," she gasps. "You're welcome. Thank you."

That was real... right?

She nods. "Yeah," she answers. "That was real."

The window panel starts to slide down. Henry scrabbles through his pockets and quickly drops another quarter in the slot. The panel slides up again; he spreads his hand and shows her the contents with a sad, wistful smile. One more quarter. He drops it in and shrugs. *How much time do we have?* he writes.

"About a minute," she answers. "Shit. You'd better get dressed."

He pulls his shirt on and zips his pants. *So is your name really Chloe?* he writes.

"No," she replies. "Of course not."

What is it really?

She gives him a long, clear look. Maybe I should make up a fake real name, she thinks. She likes this guy a lot; it'd make him happy to think she'd confided in him. She thinks carefully for a moment, then shakes her head.

"I'm not going to tell you that," she says. "I'm sorry."

Quite all right, he scribbles. *I understand. Thanks for not lying.*

"You're welcome," she replies.

They stare at each other awkwardly, somewhat at a loss for words. "That was wonderful," she says at last. "Really. You made my day."

He kisses his hand and reaches out to touch the glass. The panel drops down, sliding over his hand, clicking shut. "Come back sometime," she calls into the metal plate. She presses her hands against the window, drained and dazed and a bit forlorn, hoping that he heard her.

She feels a light touch on her shoulder. "Hey, Chloe," Tanisha says. "It's time for your break." She gives Sheila a light slap on the rump. "Nice show, girl," she adds. "Hell, you even got me going."

"Thanks," Sheila sighs. "Me, too. Sometimes I really like this job."

"I know what you mean, babe," Tanisha says as Sheila walks off the stage. "I know what you mean."

Resource Guide

GENERAL SEX INFORMATION

San Francisco Sex Information

This is probably the single most important resource available in this guide. They're a phone hotline and website providing free, non-judgmental information about all aspects of sex and sexuality. If they can't answer your question, they can probably help you find someone who can. You can call them, visit their website to see if your question is answered on their "frequent questions" page, or email them. Please bear in mind that they are not a free phone sex company, so if you just want to talk dirty to someone, please call a phone sex line instead.

www.sfsi.org

877/472-SFSI (toll-free anywhere in the U.S.)

415/989-SFSI

ask-us@sfsi.org (please read the "frequent questions" web page before emailing!)

RESOURCES FOR SEX WORK CUSTOMERS

Dickie Virgin

www.dickievirgin.com

Ads and listings for pro dommes.

Eros Guide

www.eros.com

Ads and listings for female, male, and trans escorts, pro dominants, pro submissives, etc. Listings for just about every major city in the US, and several international cities as well. They also have an online magazine, and feature articles on providers, classes, events, etc.

Max Fisch

www.maxfisch.com

Ads and listings for pro dommes.

RESOURCES FOR SEX WORKERS

Adult Industry Medical Health Care Foundation (A.I.M. Clinic)
aim-med.org
818/981-5681
aim@aim-med.org
An organization to care for the physical and emotional needs of sex workers and people in the adult entertainment industry. HIV and STD testing and treatment, counseling, and support group programs.

BAYSWAN
www.bayswan.org
415/751-1659
PO Box 210256
San Francisco, CA 94121
info@bayswan.org
This Website has links to many international sex worker advocacy groups. Provides links for major sex worker groups around the country and the world, including COYOTE, PONY, the Exotic Dancers Alliance, the Prostitutes Education Network, and all the important task forces. Maintained by sex work activist Carol Leigh, a.k.a. Scarlot Harlot.

Exotic Dancers Alliance
www.eda-sf.org
A labor organization and advocacy group for exotic dancers and other sex industry workers. Organized the first successful nude dancers' labor union, at the Lusty Lady Theater in San Francisco, and subsequently organized the employees' buyout of the theater and its conversion into a worker-owned co-operative.

St. James Infirmary
www.stjamesinfirmary.org
415/554-8494
A health clinic for sex workers in San Francisco. Free, confidential, non-judgmental medical and social services for female, transgendered, and male sex workers. The first occupational safety and health clinic for sex workers run by and for sex workers.

OTHER GOOD BOOKS ABOUT SEX WORK

Sex Work: Writings by Women in the Sex Industry. Frederique Delacoste and Priscilla Alexander, eds. The grandmama of all books on sex work. A collection of writings by street prostitutes, exotic dancers, nude models, escorts, porn stars, and massage parlor workers. This was the first book to write about sex work from the perspective of the workers themselves, without judgment, sugar-coating, or titillation.

Annie Sprinkle: Post-Porn Modernist. Annie Sprinkle. Sex worker, sex performance artist, and sex activist Annie Sprinkle writes her memoir about her life in the industry and beyond.

Chicken: Self-Portrait of a Young Man for Rent. David Henry Sterry. The story of a teenage boy in the '70s who becomes a sex worker servicing rich women in Beverly Hills.

Global Sex Workers: Rights, Resistance, and Redefinition. Kamala Kempadoo and Jo Doezema, eds. Presents the personal experiences of sex workers around the world, drawing on individual narratives. Particularly useful for its discussion of sex tourism and the experiences of sex workers and customers in other countries and cultures.

The Happy Hooker: My Own Story. Xaviera Hollander. Groundbreaking '70s memoir of a sex-positive prostitute who enjoyed her work.

I Was a Teenage Dominatrix. Shawna Kenney. Memoir of a young woman who put herself through college by working as a dominatrix.

Hustling: A Gentleman's Guide to the Fine Art of Homosexual Prostitution. John Preston. Legendary sex writer John Preston solicited the advice of working boys from across the country in his effort to produce the ultimate guide to the hustler's world.

Live Sex Acts: Women Performing Erotic Labor. Wendy Chapkis. This book captures the wide-ranging, multi-faceted experiences of women performing erotic labor. Combines scholarly analysis with personal interviews and extensive photos.

Phone Sex: Aural Thrills and Oral Skills. Miranda Austin. A phone sex worker gives advice on how to do phone sex, and shares anecdotes culled from thousands of professional phone sex calls.

Strapped for Cash: A History of American Hustler Culture. Mack Friedman. A history of male and transgendered hustler culture in America, from the 1600s to today.

Strip City: A Stripper's Farewell Journey Across America. Lily Burana. An odyssey across America with an ex-stripper who performs in strip clubs across the country in a farewell tour.

Tricks and Treats: Sex Workers Write About Their Clients. Matt Bernstein Sycamore, ed. True stories about sex work customers from male, female, and transgendered sex workers. Their commercial, cultural, emotional, sexual, (il)legal, and even spiritual relationships with their clients are discussed in detail.

Turning Pro: A Guide to Sex Work for the Ambitious and the Intrigued. Magdalene Meretrix. A manual for anybody who's ever considered a career as a phone sex operator, escort, call girl, exotic dancer, adult film performer, or any other kind of sex worker.

Whores and Other Feminists. Jill Nagle, ed. Feminist politics from the perspective of sex workers – strippers, prostitutes, porn writers, producers and performers, dominatrices – and their allies.

SEX PRODUCT COMPANIES

These are some stores and Websites where you can find books and videos with information about sex work, specific kinds of sexuality such as SM, and sexuality in general. (Most of them also carry toys and lubes and stuff to make all kinds of sexual play more fun.) Many of these business also have in-store classes on various kinds of sexuality.

Blowfish
General-interest sex products. Mail-order only.
www.blowfish.com
PO Box 41120
San Francisco CA 94141
800/325-2569
blowfish@blowfish.com

Good Vibrations
General-interest sex products.
Mail-order with retail stores and classes in San Francisco.
www.goodvibes.com
Mail-order:
800/289-8423
938 Howard Street, Suite 101
San Francisco, CA 94103
customerservice@goodvibes.com
Retail stores:
603 Valencia Street
San Francisco, CA 94110
415/522-5460
1620 Polk Street
San Francisco, CA 94109
415/345-0400

2504 San Pablo Avenue
Berkeley, CA 94702
510/841-8987

Last Gasp
Book and comic catalog with an extensive selection of sex-related material. Mail-order only.
www.lastgasp.com
800/848-4277
777 Florida Street
San Francisco, CA 94110
lastgasp@pacbell.net

Leathermasters
BDSM, leather, and fetish books and products. Mail-order with

retail stores in San Jose, Allentown, and San Antonio.
www.leathermasters.com
Mail-order:
800/417-2636 outside California
408/293-7660 in California
orders@leathermasters.com
Retail stores:
969 Park Avenue
San Jose, California 95126
408/293-7660
1023 Hamilton Street
Allentown, Pennsylvania 18101
610/434-3626
1010 N. Main Street
San Antonio, TX 78212

Mr. S/Madame S Leather
BDSM, leather, and fetish books and products. Mail-order with retail stores in San Francisco and Los Angeles.
www.mr-s-leather-fetters.com
www.madame-s.com
Mail-order:
800/746-7677
310 7th Street
San Francisco, CA 94103
hunter@mr-s-leather.com
Retail stores:
Mr. S San Francisco
310 7th Street
San Francisco, CA 94103
415/863-7764
Madame S
321 7th Street
San Francisco, CA 94103
415/863-9447
Mr. S Los Angeles
4232 Melrose Avenue
Los Angeles, CA 90029
323/663-7765

Powell's
The thinking person's alternative to Amazon.com. An enormous selection of books on every subject, including sexuality. If it's in print, they can almost certainly get it for you; if they don't have it in stock, they'll special-order it. Mail-order, with retail stores in Portland, OR.
www.powells.com
Mail-order:
800/878-7323
1005 W. Burnside
Portland, OR 97209
orders@powells.com
Flagship retail store:
1005 W. Burnside
Portland, OR 97209
800/878-7323

Toys in Babeland
General-interest sex products. Mail-order with retail stores and classes in Seattle and New York.
www.babeland.com
Mail-order:
800/658-9119
184 10th St
Oakland CA 94607
mailorder@babeland.com
Retail stores:
707 E. Pike St.
Seattle, WA 98122
206/328-2914
94 Rivington St.
New York, NY 10002
212/375-1701
43 Mercer St.
New York NY 10013
212/966-2120

Contributor Bios

STEPHANIE ANDERSON has worked as a professional dominant, BDSM purchaser, adult store clerk, waitress in a strip bar, senior investment assistant, pre-med student, and marketing assistant. This is her first published story. She hopes to do more writing.

JORGE BALÇA is a Portuguese London-based actor, director, and performing arts graduate. Currently working as a journalist, he has five years of insight and personal experience in the sex industry. He is a published author in a range of publications, with a particular interest in sexuality and queer studies.

LORD MASTER DAMIEN is a professional male dominant based in Los Angeles. Sincere submissives and/or masochists may contact him through his Website, www.MasterDamien.com.

DELICIOUS DAWN is a phone sex operator catering to the "Mature Naughty Neighbor" niche. She is also an erotic story writer with credits in *Playgirl, Hustler, Blue Food*, and more. A variety of free stories, some hot pics, and phone sex services can be found at her website, dawn.nylonfetish.org.

CLÉO DUBOIS is a BDSM educator, ritualist, and community player. Her Academy of SM Arts teaches bondage and SM to couples, dominants, and switches, both privately and in seminars, alone and in collaboration with Sybil Holiday and Chicago-based Mistress Minax. She has produced two educational/play BDSM videos, *The Pain Game* and *Tie Me Up*. She has been published in *Different Loving, Bitch Goddess*, and *Sex Tips and Tales from Women Who Dare*, as well as *Salon, On Our Backs, Skin Two*, and various online BDSM publications. For more info visit www.cleodubois.com and www.sm-arts.com.

GINGER moved up to Northern California in 1991 to attend college. Thirteen years and one college degree later (BA, Journalism, Humboldt State University, 1995), she still doesn't plan on moving away any time soon. She currently lives with her husband and three huge cats. In her off-hours between working at any one of her multiple jobs, she teaches strip-tease classes – and loves every minute of it. This is her first published piece.

NINA HARTLEY, the first self-acknowledged "feminist porn star," has been working as a public advocate for sexual self-awareness, sanity and literacy since 1983. Through her 600-plus adult videos and films, her two decades of dance tours, and her thousands of personal appearances, she has become the most enduringly popular star in the history of the medium. She was a founding member of the Feminist Anti-Censorship Task Force, and she currently lectures on campuses across the country, as well as co-producing her own line of instructional videos. Her publishing credits include *Sex Work, Whores and Other Feminists*, and *Tricks and Treats*. She currently writes advice columns for the magazines *On Our Backs* and *Hustler's Taboo*. Further information can be found at www.nina.com.

JOY JAMES divides her time between Washington DC, and New York City. Her writing has appeared in the print anthologies *Best Fetish Erotica, Erotic Travel Tales 2*, and *Naughty Stories from A to Z, Volume III*, as well as on websites such as Cleansheets and MindCaviar.

LIBERTY N. JUSTICE danced in the peepshow and entertained in the "Private Pleasures" booth at San Francisco's Lusty Lady Theater from 1990 to 1993. Since then, she has expressed her exhibitionistic tendencies in writing. Mostly.

KOKO worked as a professional S/M submissive in the San Francisco Bay Area in the early 1990s. She does like how men smell. Up to a point.

JESSICA MELUSINE holds two M.A. degrees in English literature. In addition to working as a phone fantasy operator, she has taught at the college level, and worked as a tech writer and an adult model. Her fiction has appeared in *Shameless: Women's Intimate Erotica, Zaftig: Well Rounded Erotica*, and is forthcoming in *Glamour Girls: Femme/Femme Erotica*. As a model, she has appeared on Faeriefantasies.com, Sssspread.com, and Thatstrangegirl.com. She likes eighteenth-century literature, ceremonial magick, sacred whoredom, amateur folklore, expensive lipstick, and cheap champagne; to learn more, please visit her at www.jessicamelusine.com.

MAGDALENE MERETRIX is the author of *Turning Pro: A Guide to Sex Work for the Ambitious and the Intrigued,* and author/performer of the spoken word erotica album *Eloquent Perversions* (available through her website). In addition to having authored dozens of articles, essays, and short stories, Magdalene is also a musician, textile artist, Web designer, mathematician, sharp-shooter, and veteran of 18 years in various fields within the sex industry, ranging from phone sex operator to professional submissive to legal prostitute. She grew up in Dixie and now lives among the elk and tumbleweed in the Wild West. Visit her website at www.magdalenemeretrix.com.

JENNIFER MILLIS is a performance artist, writer, and dancer whose work strives to implode classic and modern form and create social change. "How to Find Your Inner Gentleman..." is her first published feature, but you can often find her reading at open mics around town. A former stripper and sex worker, she now spends most of her time writing and dancing with her clothes on. A member of Diamond Daggers Burlesque Troupe and soon to start her own company, she still hasn't stopped shaking her groove thang. Millis is a graduate of UC Berkeley's Literature program and City College's dance certificate program. She lives in San Francisco.

STEVE MITCHELL has been working as a stripper for ten years, and considers himself a veteran of the business. He also works as a personal trainer. He lives and works in the San Francisco area. His agency is Barely Legal Entertainment; their website is www.menofca.com, and they're in the Yellow Pages. He guarantees you won't be disappointed.

VERONICA MONET is a sex educator who offers professional advice on sex and relationships, and gives lectures such as Ten Things a Woman Should Never Do for Free and The Truth About Men. Monet is published in *Human Sexuality: Opposing Viewpoints; Whores and Other Feminists; Breaking Ritual Silence;* and *Porn 101.* Her television credits include CNN, A&E, ABC's 20/20, Fox News and Bill Maher's Politically Incorrect. She has a B.S. in Psychology; training in Tantra, Human Sexuality, and Ancient Sacred Prostitution; and over a decade's experience as an erotic model, porn actress, prostitute, escort, and courtesan. Her website is www.veronicamonet.com.

MISTRESS MORGANA is an experienced San Francisco-based professional dominant and sex educator. Her workshops on BDSM have delighted thousands of kink-curious people of all persuasions, and she is the co-writer and host of the instructional video *Whipsmart: A Good*

Vibrations Guide to SM for Beginning Couples. To learn more, visit www.mistressmorgana.com.

CAROL QUEEN got a doctorate in sexology while she was doing sex work – in fact, without sex work, doubtless there would have been no doctorate. She's a much-published and award-winning author and editor and has also appeared in a number of sex education videos. For a complete list of her writing, plus articles and stuff, visit www.carolqueen.com. She's a longtime worker/owner at Good Vibrations and regularly writes for the GV Magazine at www.goodvibes.com.

MR. SLEEP is the working name of Vincent Rose, grand pajandrum of Mack Avenue Skullgame. He can be contacted through www.skullgame.com.

ANNIE SPRINKLE worked as a massage parlor prostitute for twenty years, and came out a winner. She recently became the first porn star to get a Ph.D. She is currently editing her newest film, *Orgasm – A Documentary,* and is writing *Your Sex Life Makeover – 10 Steps to a Spectacular Sex Life,* to be published by Penguin/Tarcher. She lives in sexy Sin Francisco with her domestic partner Beth Stephens, and has never been happier. Next year she'll be 50 years old and feels that the best is yet to come. Visit her website at www.anniesprinkle.org.

VIC ST. BLAISE, a.k.a. Lex Kyler, turned his first trick on San Francisco's infamous Polk Street, in the days before the dot com boom, and continues to work in the sex industry today. He birthed the sex worker 'zine *Whorezine* in the early '90s, joined COYOTE, PONY, and ISWFACE, and sat on the San Francisco Task Force on Prostitution. He has been involved in a number of activist causes and is likely the first porn star to start a rugby team.

MATTILDA, a.k.a. Matt Bernstein Sycamore, is the author of the novel *Pulling Taffy,* as well as the editor of two non-fiction anthologies – *Tricks and Treats: Sex Workers Write About Their Clients,* and *Dangerous Families: Queer Writing on Surviving.* He is an instigator of Gay Shame: The Virus in the System, the radical queer activist group that fights the monster of assimilation. He is currently at work on a second novel, as well as a new anthology, *Resisting Assimilation: Alternatives to the Gay Mainstream.* Visit www.mattbernsteinsycamore.com.

TALIESIN THE BARD is a popular part-time porn performer, pagan pundit, practicing polyamorist, and prominent prosex partisan, as well as being addicted to atrocious alliteration. Tal has used his porn popularity to propel himself into a full-fledged literary career, writing novels, short stories, and comic books. *Starfox,* his sci-fi sensation, can be seen on www.ambassadorstarfox.com and in a recently published short story collection. Visit Tal on the Web at www.taliesinthebard.com and www.firsttribebooks.com.

SERENA LUCINE VERSEAU wrote her first play, *Vanitia Metropolita,* at age 17, and presented it at San Francisco's Bannam Place Theater. She moved to Paris, learned French, and performed her award-winning plays, *Aigre Est Le Vin* and *La Patte Du Serpent,* at the infamous Cours Florent. Serena has appeared in a plethora of Bay Area poetry readings, during which time she produced a collection entitled *Mandala* (Eyelet Press) and a metaphysical manifesto, *Ascension Soliloquy* (Apocalypse Press). Her fiction, philosophy, journalism, plays, poems and songs appear in anthologies, magazines, newspapers, CDs, radio, television and film all across the subterranean cavity. She is currently working on her novel, *The Discarnates.*

SAGE VIVANT operates Custom Erotica Source, the online resource for tailor-made erotic fiction. Her stories have been published in numerous anthologies, from *Best Women's Erotica* to *The Mammoth Book of Best New Erotica,* and she is a frequent guest on radio and television shows. She is the author of *29 Ways to Write Great Erotica* (www.29eroticways.com), editor of the anthology *Swing!,* and co-editor with M. Christian of *Binary: Bisexual Erotica* and *Leather, Lace, and Lust.* Visit Custom Erotica Source at www.customeroticasource.com.

MISTRESS SIMONE WORTHINGTON has been a professional domina for the last 10 years. Her focus is on the spiritual transformation one experiences through the exploration of their fetishism. Currently a graduate student doing research within the BDSM lifestyle, she seeks to encourage non-leather people to explore their darker sexuality. She has spent the last seven years as manager of The Leather Rose, a BDSM social club in Chicago. For the last two years she has been Executive Director of the LRA, a not-for-profit leather organization. She currently resides in Chicago with her leather household and three cats. She can be reached at www.chicago-mistress.com.

Author Bio

Greta Christina has been writing professionally since 1989. Her writing has appeared in numerous magazines and newspapers, including *Ms.* and *Penthouse,* as well as several anthologies, including *Best Ameri-*

can Erotica 2003. Her influential essay "Are We Having Sex Now Or What?" has been reprinted several times and has been studied and cited by scholars, writers and universities throughout the country. Her erotic novella, *Bending*, edited by Susie Bright, is scheduled for publication by Simon & Schuster in Summer 2005. She worked as a peep show dancer at the Lusty Lady Theater in 1989, and as the lead buyer for a mail-order sex products company from 1996 to 2002. She lives in San Francisco, where her longtime partner/recent wife also resides. You can visit her website at www.gretachristina.com. This is her first book.

OTHER BOOKS FROM GREENERY PRESS

GENERAL SEXUALITY

Big Big Love: A Sourcebook on Sex for People of Size and Those Who Love Them
Hanne Blank $15.95

The Bride Wore Black Leather... And He Looked Fabulous!: An Etiquette Guide for the Rest of Us
Andrew Campbell $11.95

The Ethical Slut: A Guide to Infinite Sexual Possibilities
Dossie Easton & Catherine A. Liszt $16.95

A Hand in the Bush: The Fine Art of Vaginal Fisting
Deborah Addington $13.95

Health Care Without Shame: A Handbook for the Sexually Diverse and Their Caregivers
Charles Moser, Ph.D., M.D. $11.95

Look Into My Eyes: How to Use Hypnosis to Bring Out the Best in Your Sex Life
Peter Masters $16.95

Phone Sex: Oral Thrills and Aural Skills
Miranda Austin $15.95

Photography for Perverts
Charles Gatewood $27.95

Sex Disasters... And How to Survive Them
Charles Moser, Ph.D., M.D. and Janet W. Hardy $16.95

Tricks... To Please a Man
Tricks... To Please a Woman
both by Jay Wiseman $14.95 ea.

Turning Pro: A Guide to Sex Work for the Ambitious and the Intrigued
Magdalene Meretrix $16.95

When Someone You Love Is Kinky
Dossie Easton & Catherine A. Liszt $15.95

BDSM/KINK

The Compleat Spanker
Lady Green $12.95

Erotic Tickling
Michael Moran $13.95

Family Jewels: A Guide to Male Genital Play and Torment
Hardy Haberman $12.95

Flogging
Joseph W. Bean $12.95

Intimate Invasions: The Ins and Outs of Erotic Enema Play
M.R. Strict $13.95

Jay Wiseman's Erotic Bondage Handbook
Jay Wiseman $16.95

The Kinky Girl's Guide to Dating
Luna Grey $16.95

The Loving Dominant
John Warren $16.95

Miss Abernathy's Concise Slave Training Manual
Christina Abernathy $12.95

The Mistress Manual
Mistress Lorelei $16.95

The Sexually Dominant Woman: A Workbook for Nervous Beginners
Lady Green $11.95

SM 101: A Realistic Introduction
Jay Wiseman $24.95

Training With Miss Abernathy: A Workbook for Erotic Slaves and Their Owners
Christina Abernathy $13.95

TOYBAG GUIDES: A Workshop In A Book
$9.95 each

Canes and Caning, by Janet Hardy

Clips and Clamps, by Jack Rinella

Hot Wax and Temperature Play, by Spectrum

Dungeon Emergencies & Supplies, by Jay Wiseman

FICTION

... But I Know What You Want: 25 Sex Tales for the Different
James Williams $13.95

Love, Sal: letters from a boy in The City
Sal Iacopelli, ill. Phil Foglio $13.95

Murder At Roissy
John Warren $15.95

Haughty Spirit
The Warrior Within
The Warrior Enchained
all by Sharon Green $11.95 ea.

Please include $3 for first book and $1 for each additional book with your order to cover shipping and handling costs, plus $10 for overseas orders. VISA/MC accepted. Order from Greenery Press, 4200 Park Blvd. pmb 240, Oakland, CA 510/652-2596